Praise for Elizabeth Bevarly:

"...supersteamy..."
—*Cosmopolitan*

"...fresh and funny."
—*Publishers Weekly*

"...the very best in love and laughter."
—*Romantic Times*

"Practically perfect romance..."
—*Library Journal*

"Elizabeth Bevarly delivers romantic
comedy at its sparkling best!"
—Bestselling author Teresa Medeiros

"I just love Elizabeth Bevarly's sense of humor."
—Bestselling author Julia Quinn

Don't miss Signature Select's exciting series:

The Fortunes of Texas: Reunion

**Starting in June 2005, get swept up in
twelve new stories from your favorite family!**

COWBOY AT MIDNIGHT by Ann Major

A BABY CHANGES EVERYTHING by Marie Ferrarella

IN THE ARMS OF THE LAW by Peggy Moreland

LONE STAR RANCHER by Laurie Paige

THE GOOD DOCTOR by Karen Rose Smith

THE DEBUTANTE by Elizabeth Bevarly

KEEPING HER SAFE by Myrna Mackenzie

THE LAW OF ATTRACTION by Kristi Gold

ONCE A REBEL by Sheri WhiteFeather

MILITARY MAN by Marie Ferrarella

FORTUNE'S LEGACY by Maureen Child

THE RECKONING by Christie Ridgway

THE FORTUNES OF TEXAS: Reunion

ELIZABETH BEVARLY
The Debutante

Published by Silhouette Books
America's Publisher of Contemporary Romance

Special thanks and acknowledgment are given to Elizabeth Bevarly for her contribution to THE FORTUNES OF TEXAS: REUNION series.

 SILHOUETTE BOOKS

THE DEBUTANTE

Copyright © 2005 by Harlequin Books S.A.

ISBN 0-373-38931-0

Visit Silhouette Books at www.eHarlequin.com

Printed in U.S.A.

Dear Reader,

Writing continuities for Silhouette is always so much fun. First, there's the challenge of taking the story and characters the editors create and making them my own, and then there's the joy of working with so many of my favorite writers. I was both flattered and delighted to be invited to participate in THE FORTUNES OF TEXAS: REUNION. *The Debutante* is my second contribution to the Fortunes saga, and it was wonderful to be able to go back and visit the family again. I had a terrific time writing about Lanie and Miles, and about their sometimes rocky, sometimes comical, journey toward finding true love. I hope you have fun reading about them, too.

Happy Reading!

Elizabeth Bevarly

For the readers.
With a million billion thanks.

One

No carrot cake. Drat. She'd just have to settle for chocolate torte instead.

Lanie Meyers sighed with not-quite-heartfelt disappointment at the realization. Ah, well. One couldn't have everything, could one? Not even at a "Dessert, the Whole Dessert, and Nothing But Dessert" fund-raiser for one's own father's gubernatorial campaign.

Not that Lanie understood the need for yet another fundraiser, even if it did involve the consumption of mass quantities of sugar. Her father was already governor of Texas, and last she heard, he was still ahead in the polls, even if it was only by a small margin. And since October was nearly over, the election was less than two weeks away. She just didn't see how a last-minute financial push like this was going to help all that much. Nevertheless, if her father's campaign wanted to host a $100-per-person party at this point in the game, the least Lanie could do was show up for it.

And eat lots and lots of dessert.

She scooped up a modest serving of the chocolate torte—well, okay, maybe it wasn't as modest as some—and transferred it to her plate. Then, just to be on the safe side, she forked up a little—kind of—piece of what looked like marble pound cake to go with it. And, okay, just a smallish—sort of—piece of the maple nut cake, too. It just really complemented the other two so nicely, aesthetically speaking. And maybe just a teeny slice of the white velvet cake to fill in that last empty spot on her plate.

Well, she'd written a check to her father's campaign for a hundred dollars just like everyone else here tonight had. There was no reason why Lanie shouldn't enjoy as much of the spread as the other guests. Besides, she'd been forced to skip dinner because her mother had wanted her to come along for moral support during the speech Luanne Meyers had given to the Austin Gardening Society. Lanie just decided not to think for now about how snug her clothes would feel in the morning. That was tomorrow, after all. Fiddle-de-dee on that. She told herself it was only her imagination that the brief, strapless sapphire-blue cocktail dress she'd donned for the occasion was already beginning to pinch.

Nudging away a stray lock of blond hair that had fallen into her face from the topknot fixed loosely at the crown of her head, she retrieved her glass of club soda from where she had left it on the table, took her mile-high pile of assorted cakes and retreated to the far side of the room where she could eat in peace, removed from the crowd. The ballroom of the Four Seasons Austin was packed with her father's supporters, the majority of them talking politics, naturally, which was probably Lanie's least favorite topic of conversation in the entire world. She would have rather talked about the mating habits of the luna moth, for heaven's sake. Unfortunately, she being the daughter of a Texas governor, it seemed as if everyone assumed she was as rabid about state government as Tom Meyers was. There were even a few of her father's cronies who had dropped hints that Lanie herself might run for office one day.

As if.

She could think of scores of occupations she'd rather pursue than stateswoman. Of course, there were those who might argue that her current occupation was hobnobber, which wasn't that far off from politician.

Lanie just hadn't figured out yet what she wanted to do with her life, that was all. Yes, at twenty-five she probably should have some vague notion of what path she wanted to follow—professionally, if nothing else. But she'd been groomed since childhood to be the daughter of a politician, and no one had ever encouraged her to stray from that path. Even in college, Lanie had majored in fine arts, not exactly a field of study that had made her highly employable. But she'd volunteered on both of her father's gubernatorial campaigns, and she worked side by side with her mother in a number of charitable organizations, so she did stay busy. Income wasn't exactly a problem, since the Meyerses were quite wealthy, and Lanie was what had commonly become referred to as a "trust-fund baby."

Nevertheless, there were days when even she was appalled by her lack of contribution to the working world. Not that she wanted to set the world on fire or anything, but a person liked to think she was valuable somewhere, to someone, in some capacity.

No sooner had the thought unrolled in her head than Lanie glanced up from her plate to see someone very valuable indeed standing head and shoulders above a small group of people roughly twenty feet to her right. A member of the Fortune family, she realized, not at all surprised to find at least one of them in attendance tonight. Everyone in Texas knew who the Fortunes were, since they were one of the premier families of the state. It was only natural that they'd have an interest in state politics. And Lanie knew her father was presenting Ryan Fortune with the prestigious Hensley-Robinson Award later this month to honor and commemorate his many charitable contributions and volunteerism. The family no doubt wanted to reciprocate by showing their support for his campaign.

And how nice of them to send one of the yummy Fortune triplets as ambassador, Lanie thought. And how appropriate, too, since she herself had been a supporter of the Fortune triplets since she was a teenager. Just not in any political capacity.

Forget swooning over Leonardo and River in *Tiger Beat* and *Teen People*. Lanie, like so many Texas females her age, had found the Fortune triplets infinitely more worthy of admiration. She could remember more than one slumber party where copies of the newspaper and other local publications had been passed around so that all the girls could take turns cooing over photographs and stories about Steven, Clyde and Miles Fortune. Back then, the triplets were in their early twenties, eleven years older than Lanie and her friends. But everyone knew older men were so much more sophisticated and interesting than boys of twelve or thirteen. And the Fortune triplets had appealed to women of all ages.

Lanie did some quick math. She was twenty-five, so the triplets would be thirty-six now. She wondered which of the three she was looking at. Steven and Clyde, she'd read, had both recently married. But Miles, as far as she knew, was still free and clear. Not that she had any intention of approaching whichever Fortune this was, of course.

"Lanie, darling, there you are."

At the sound of her name, Lanie glanced in the opposite direction to see her mother striding toward her, and she smiled. Although Lanie had inherited her parents' blue eyes and blond hair, it was her mother she truly favored. But where Lanie's hair was long and straight and golden blond, Luanne Meyers wore her tresses bobbed at chin length, and there was an equal amount of silver mingling with the gold these days.

The two women were also nearly an identical height— five feet six inches—and both wore the same dress size— eight. Not that they ever swapped outfits, even though Lanie lived with her parents at the governor's mansion. Her mother's taste in clothing was way too traditional and much too conservative, as befitted a Texas governor's wife. Lanie certainly couldn't see herself dressed in the pale, shapeless sheaths her mother favored, like the pearl-pink one she wore tonight, with no decoration and almost no jewelry. Lanie was much better suited to her little blue dress, and she had deliberately accessorized its plain design with flash and dazzle, in the form of a spectacular crystal necklace and chandelier earrings that glittered like diamonds when she stepped into the brighter lights of the ballroom.

It wasn't that Lanie was ostentatious. But she did rather enjoy being the center of attention. Just not when she was shoveling cake into her mouth. Hence, her temporary retreat to the darker regions of the ballroom.

But her mother had found her, in spite of her efforts to remain hidden, Lanie thought. And there were a number of photographers from the press in attendance. Probably standing around pushing cake into her mouth wasn't such a good idea, all things considered. The last thing she wanted was to have some huge photo of herself showing up in the tabloids, her mouth wide open to accept an enormous gobble of cake. So, reluctantly, Lanie surrendered her still-half-full plate to the empty tray of a passing waiter. And she watched in wistful silence as he carried away the chocolate torte she hadn't even tasted. Maybe, she thought, if no one was looking, she could fill a to-go box before leaving.

"Hello, Mother," she said as Luanne Meyers drew nearer. Automatically, Lanie turned her cheek to receive her mother's kiss, then dutifully kissed her mother's cheek in return.

"Are you enjoying yourself?" her mother asked.

Without even realizing she was doing it, Lanie turned to look at her Fortune again. Whichever triplet it was continued to converse with one of the men in the group, and she smiled as she watched him. Oh, yes. She was enjoying herself very much.

She nodded in response to her mother's question, then surreptitiously tilted her head toward the man she had been observing. "Do you know which Fortune triplet that is?" she asked.

Her mother followed Lanie's gaze, and she smiled, too, when she found her target. Even her mother's generation wasn't immune to the triplets' handsomeness, Lanie thought.

"I believe that's Miles," her mother said, turning back to Lanie. "He's a friend of Dennis's."

Dennis Stovall, her father's campaign manager, Lanie translated.

"Plus, you can tell by the dimple," her mother added. "For some reason, Miles is the only one of the three boys who has it."

Ah, yes, the dimple, Lanie thought. The utterly adorable, swoonworthy dimple. She turned to look at the man again, just as he was throwing his head back to laugh. Yep. There it was. That was Miles Fortune, for sure. And he was utterly adorable. Not to mention swoonworthy.

As if she'd just spoken the thought loud enough for him to hear, he suddenly glanced over and met her gaze. His eyes widened for a split second, as if he were surprised to find himself being watched. Then he smiled, which brought out that luscious dimple again, and lifted his wineglass toward Lanie, as if toasting her. She blushed, but she wasn't sure whether it was because he'd caught her ogling him, or because he was flirting with her, or because of the errant thoughts that suddenly exploded in her brain. Unable to help herself, though, she smiled back and lifted her own glass of club soda in silent salute.

My brush with fame, she thought. Sharing a smile and a silent toast with Miles Fortune. The sad thing was, even that minuscule contact was enough that it would probably sustain her for the rest of her life. She really did need to get out more and meet people. Male people. Male people who might eventually come to mean more to her than someone with whom to have a good time.

It wasn't that Lanie was shallow. And it wasn't that she feared commitment. But her upbringing and lifestyle hadn't exactly lent themselves to forming long-standing, serious relationships. Not with the opposite sex. Not with anyone, really.

Of course, much of that was probably due to the fact that her father had spent virtually Lanie's entire life building a political career with his wife at his side, something that had prevented both him and Luanne from being the kind of parents Lanie would have liked them to be. It wasn't that her parents hadn't been attentive and affectionate when they *were* around—they had been. The times Lanie had spent in their company had always been wonderful. Those times had just ended too soon.

So Lanie had never been good at establishing and maintaining sturdy relationships with other people. And she hadn't exactly been molded into the most responsible, reliable person, either. She'd just never known what it meant to have boundaries. Since no one had ever really said no to her while she was growing up, she had always been one to act on whim. Hey, why not? No one had ever told her she couldn't.

So when she was five years old and had wanted a kitten, she'd brought one home from a neighbor's litter and had kept it hidden in her room…until the smell from the closet alerted the housekeeper to the animal's presence. Well, how was Lanie supposed to know kittens needed a litter box?

And when she was ten and had decided after bedtime one night that she wanted to spend the night with her friend Susan, she'd packed her backpack and crept down the stairs so as not to wake her nanny—her parents, of course, hadn't been at home—then she'd ridden her bike the two miles to Susan's house. Well, how was she supposed to know the nanny would be frantic about her disappearance? The woman wasn't even supposed to know she was gone!

And when she was fifteen and had figured it was time to learn to drive a car, she'd gotten into her daddy's convertible and started driving. Well, how was she supposed to know how to work a stick shift? Crashing through the garage door that way could have happened to anyone!

Regardless of how often Lanie had found herself in a bind, though, her father had always been there to bail her out of it, one way or another. Either he'd used his money or his influence—or both—and somehow, the problem just always went away. Looking back, Lanie supposed it had just been easier and less time-consuming for her father to do that than to sit down and talk with his daughter and try to help her learn from her mistakes. He was a very busy man, after all. He had a lot of important things to do. And a lot of important places to go. And a lot of important people to meet. He took his obligations very seriously.

Unlike Lanie, who was never serious for a minute. Life was for living, however she wanted to live it. She'd decided a long time ago that she'd just do what she wanted when she wanted to do it, and she'd never be serious for a moment.

Unfortunately, no one tended to take a person like that seriously. So any romantic relationships Lanie had over the years ended up being frivolous. Oh, sure, she always liked the guys she got involved with—one or two of them she'd even loved for a little while—and she always had a good time with them. But that was all those associations ever were—a good time. Of course, some had ended on a sour note when Lanie found out the guy's only interest in her was as a conduit to her father or her family fortune. But even those guys had been surprisingly easy to get over.

Fun. That was all Lanie had ever wanted out of life. And

that was all she ever really looked for. And invariably, in one way or another, she found it.

Now Luanne Meyers caught Lanie's free hand in her own, bringing her daughter's attention back around to where she was standing. "There's someone here tonight who wants to talk to you," her mother told her, her eyes fairly sparkling with glee, her lips turning up at the ends with just the hint of a secret smile.

Uh-oh, Lanie thought. The last time her mother's eyes had sparkled like that, it had been because she was about to introduce her daughter to an eighty-two-year-old millionaire rancher who'd just buried his fifth wife.

"Um, who?" Lanie asked warily.

"Oneida Steadmore-Duckworth," her mother told her, beaming.

Yikes, Lanie thought. Oneida Steadmore-Duckworth was the chairwoman of the annual Women of the Lone Star charity auction. If she wanted to talk to Lanie, it was because she wanted to put her on a committee of some kind. And Lanie had hit her committee quota for the year, thank you very much. Six months ago, as a matter of fact.

"Tell her I'll be right there," Lanie said. "I need to go to the ladies' room first and make myself presentable."

It was only a small lie, she consoled herself. After three club sodas, she did, without question, need to go to the ladies' room. And she did doubtless need to make herself presentable, since she'd been pigging out on desserts for the last half hour. And she would certainly be right there—only after Mrs. Steadmore-Duckworth had moved on to another unsuspecting victim.

Before excusing herself from her mother, Lanie stole another glance in the direction of Miles Fortune, only to find that he had disappeared. She scanned the crowd for some sign of him, but he was gone.

Ah, well, she thought. Easy come, easy go.

Scurrying off to the ladies' room, Lanie took her time seeing to her various needs. Then she tucked a few errant strands of hair back into the topknot and adjusted the shoulder-length tendrils that dangled free. She applied a fresh layer of Rouge Rage to her mouth and dabbed at a smudge of eyeliner beneath her lashes. She tugged her little blue dress back into place and smoothed a hand over the silky, barely there fabric. Then she glanced at her diamond wristwatch and sighed.

Damn. It had only been ten minutes since she'd left her mother. No way would Mrs. Steadmore-Duckworth be put off yet. That woman was tenacious when it came to organizing committees. Now Lanie was going to have to go to the extra trouble of "accidentally" getting lost on her way back to the ballroom.

Exiting the ladies' room, she veered right when she should have turned left to get back to the ballroom and made her way down a hallway identical to the one she had traveled after leaving the ballroom. Gee, if she wasn't careful, she really would get lost, she thought. She'd never realized how big this hotel was, or how so many parts of it resembled so many other parts of it. Maybe this wasn't such a good idea after all....

Miles Fortune couldn't believe he'd allowed himself to be dragged to a $100-a-plate fund-raiser where the focal point of the event was dessert. And not normal dessert like apple pie or peach cobbler or chocolate chip cookies, either. Now, had it been a bourbon whiskey tasting, he could

understand going to all the trouble and expense. But truf-
fles? Tiramisu? Sorbet? Soufflé? What the hell kind of
self-respecting male attended an event where such words
were commonplace, without even putting on a disguise and
assuming a fake name first?

And why did desserts have such sissy names to begin
with? Miles wondered further as he looked around. Even
a perfectly good word like *punch* got ruined at an event like
this by having someone put the word *fruit* in front of it. If
he ruled the world, after-dinner fare would have names like
Cherry Flamethrower or Coconut Jackhammer or good
old-fashioned Rocky Road. Hell, where was a good beer
pie when you needed one?

"Miles, you must try the chocolate bombe."

Yeah, Chocolate Bomb, that'd be a good one, too, he
thought. Oh, wait. Evidently, that was one.

He turned to the woman who had just suggested it,
Jenny Stovall, who'd been on the planning committee of
the event. She was also the woman who'd roped Miles
into attending it. Her husband, Dennis, was Governor
Meyers's campaign manager, and a friend of Miles's
from college. Jenny, Miles saw, was busily sampling one
of everything she'd been able to get her hands on. But
since the normally petite brunette was seven months
pregnant with twins, and therefore eating for three, he
supposed it wasn't unexpected that she would have
enough food on her plate for six. Or maybe it was just
that her serving of chocolate bomb had exploded all over
everything else.

"What the hell is a chocolate bomb?" he asked warily,
just in case it did have the potential to detonate.

"Not sure," Jenny said. "Ice cream, though, for certain.

And chocolate, of course. This white stuff seems to be whipped cream. Have some. You'll love it."

"I'd rather look for the bar," he said, gazing at his still-full wineglass and thinking that a bourbon whiskey tasting would be pretty good about now. "The real bar, I mean. Not one of the ones they set up for this thing. Those don't serve what a man likes to drink. Not a Texan, anyway." No, all those bars had were wine and champagne and stuff in triangular-shaped glasses that were pale, pretty colors Miles didn't want to get within fifty feet of.

"The real bar is through the far exit," Jenny told him without breaking stride in her eating, waving her fork airily toward the other side of the room. "To the right and down a ways."

Miles eyed her suspiciously. "You know, Jenny, it occurs to me that a woman who's seven months pregnant with twins shouldn't know where the bar is."

"Of course she should," Jenny countered, "when that's where the closest women's room is."

Miles supposed that would mean something to another woman—especially another pregnant woman—and manfully decided not to dwell on it himself. Instead, he took Jenny's directions to heart, and after making sure she had someone else to talk to, he excused himself and wandered off in that direction. As he went, he found himself scanning the crowd, looking for someone. A female someone, to be precise. A female someone with blond hair twisted onto the top of her head in a way that made a man's fingers itch to loosen it, and with eyes that were as blue and enormous as her dress was blue and tiny.

He wondered who the young woman was with whom he'd shared an impromptu toast. And he wondered why he was still thinking about her now, a full fifteen minutes after the fact. Out of sight usually meant out of mind for Miles when it came to women. He was a firm believer in the "If you can't be with the one you love, love the one you're with" philosophy. Probably mostly because he'd never been in love. Not a heart-stopping, storybook, ever-after kind of love, anyway. So loving the one he was with was about as good as it got for him.

Tonight, however, for this occasion, he wasn't with anyone. Which meant his recent, brief, if silent, exchange with the blonde was, for now, the equivalent to a love that would span all time.

As he threaded his way carefully through the crowd, Miles wondered where she might have gone. She'd looked the way he felt—out of his element—and that as much as anything, he supposed, had cemented a weird sort of bond between them. He knew he shouldn't feel uncomfortable here, though. He was a Fortune, after all, and no stranger to wealth and refinement. And God knew, he'd always been one to jump at any excuse to party.

But Miles wasn't much one for the political crowd. Sure, he cared about his country and the great state of Texas, but both had been moving along just fine for centuries without his input and would continue to do so for centuries after he was gone. He figured that as long as he was reading the newspaper regularly to keep himself informed and voting his conscience every time election day came around, then he was doing his civic duty. He'd just leave the actual running of things to the people who knew more about it than he did.

But he'd been in Austin on business this weekend and had, as he always did, made plans to see Dennis and Jenny while he was in town. This event for the governor was too big a deal for either of them to miss, though, so Miles had agreed to meet them here instead of for dinner somewhere, which was their normal arrangement. Once Jenny delivered those twins, she and Dennis weren't going to have a lot of free time to do things like dinner out with their still blissfully single and delightedly child-free friends.

He smiled at the thought of his friend Dennis becoming a dad. The guy was suited to it. In fact, Miles wondered why he and Jenny hadn't done this years ago. He admired the two of them for their commitment to each other and to the family they were creating, but he didn't understand it for a minute. Not that Miles didn't think family was important. He *was* a Fortune, after all, and to the Fortunes, family was everything.

He hadn't always known that, though. His grandfather, Mark Fortune, had estranged himself from the rest of the Fortune clan years ago, both literally and figuratively. And Miles had done most of his growing up in New York, where his parents had moved before he was born so that his father could pursue a career in finance, and Patrick and Lacey both could work for the social and political causes they felt passionately about. By the time Miles had hit adolescence, however, his parents had reunited with the rest of the Fortune clan, and Miles and Steven and Clyde had begun spending every summer in Texas. It was those summers here that had caused the three boys to fall in love with the place, and when they'd come of age, they'd invested together in the Flying Aces, a modest ranch near Red Rock.

Steven, however, still feeling restless, had struck out on his own and purchased his own spread, which had only recently become habitable, outside Austin. That was where he and his new wife, Amy, were living now. But Miles and Clyde still called the Flying Aces home. And so did Clyde's new wife, Jessica. Fortunately, the main house was large and separated into suites for each of the triplets. Clyde and Jessica had their own space in one part of the house, and Miles had his in another. Which was good, because he had a feeling Clyde and Jessica were already talking about starting a family.

But Miles didn't have any desire to grow his own branch on the family tree, even in light of the way that tree suddenly seemed to be leafing out. Not only were two thirds of the triplets now committed to matrimony, but their sister Violet was engaged, too. And their oldest brother, Jack, had just married recently and settled in Texas. There was no way, however, that Miles would be upholding that particular family tradition. He was having too much fun as a single man. And he didn't want to be responsible for anyone but himself.

He found the bar easily enough after following Jenny's directions, and ordered a bourbon straight up. Restless, though, he didn't feel like sitting at the bar and drinking alone. But he didn't feel like returning to the fund-raiser, either. Wrapping his fingers around the heavy glass tumbler, he turned—

—and saw a flash of sapphire-blue speeding past the bar's entrance on the other side of the room.

Instinctively, Miles headed toward the door and walked through it, just in time to see that flash of blue disappear around a corner at the end of the hall. And although he couldn't be positive, he was pretty sure there had been a blond topknot attached to the woman wearing it.

In a word, *hmm*…

There was a glass-enclosed sunroom at the end of that hallway, he knew. And it had been a nice evening, cool and crisp and cloudless, when he'd arrived at the hotel. No doubt it had turned into one of those crystal-clear nights by now, the kind where the constellations were all very easy to find.

Yeah, he thought as his fingers wrapped more firmly around his glass and he began to walk in the same direction as the blue dress, maybe a little stroll would do him good....

Two

Okay, she was well and truly lost now, no mistaking *or* faking it. As Lanie stood in the middle of a darkened sunroom, gazing at the inky, star-spattered sky through the glass ceiling overhead, she asked herself where she could have possibly gone wrong.

Probably, she immediately answered herself, it was when she had decided to deliberately avoid Mrs. Steadmore-Duckworth by telling her mother a fib.

Bad karma will out.

Still, her bad karma couldn't be all *that* bad, she decided, since it had led her to a room that was quiet, reflective and pretty, a welcome contrast to the noisy, bustling, extravagant party she'd just left. She hesitated before turning around to leave, attracted to the almost Zen-like serenity of the sunroom. It was more than a little appealing for someone who had survived as hectic a day as Lanie had.

Maybe she should just take advantage of a peaceful moment and enjoy it for a few minutes before venturing back to the raucous fund-raiser.

At night like this, the sunroom was really more of a moon room. And the moon was indeed visible, shining like a newly minted silver dollar smack-dab in the middle of the dark sky above. Beyond and around it, stars glittered like tiny gemstones. If Lanie focused very hard, she thought she could see the milky gleam of the galaxy threading its way through the darkness, too. Tables and chairs dotted the room, unused at the moment, but their glass hurricane centerpieces winked in the moonlight as if a few stray stars had spilled into them. Here and there, along the perimeter of the room, pots of ferns and trailing bougainvillea hung from what, in the dim light, appeared to be magic. Coupled with the night sky above, the view made Lanie feel as if she had stumbled into a lush, deserted jungle. The only thing that prevented the impression from gelling completely was that somewhere behind her she could hear the faint strains of jazz—something soft and mellow and perfect for the nighttime hours, the metallic swish of brushes on drum skins inciting an echoing purr of delight that rumbled up from somewhere deep inside her.

It wasn't easy being a jazz fan in Texas, where country and western and southern-fried rock reigned. Someone here at the Four Seasons must like it, too, she thought. Or maybe her karma really wasn't so bad after all, and the Fates had simply seen fit to reward her for some good deed she couldn't remember doing.

For another long moment, Lanie only stood in the center of the deserted sunroom, gazing up at the sky, enjoying the soft sound of music. What was the harm? By now, her mother would have decided she'd been waylaid by another partygoer and would be promising Mrs. Steadmore-Duckworth that she'd make sure her daughter called her first thing in the morning. And Lanie would, she silently promised, her guilty conscience gnawing at her. She could fit one more committee into her year, provided it was for a good cause. It was the least she could do for Mrs. Steadmore-Duckworth, since avoiding the woman had given Lanie a few moments of peace and quiet in an otherwise turbulent world.

Funny how rewards came out of nowhere sometimes. Good thing she had the good sense to enjoy it.

Not sure what compelled her to do it, Lanie strode to the other side of the room, halting between an especially dense fern and an especially fragrant bougainvillea. Gazing through the window, she thought she caught a glimpse of movement outside, in the bushes that lay just beyond the glass. She noticed then that the entire sunroom was surrounded by outdoor greenery, which, like the potted plants inside, added to the exotic feel of the place. No doubt something small and hungry was out there scavenging about, she thought. Though she doubted it was any more exotic than an armadillo. She placed her open hand against the cool glass of the window, spreading her fingers wide in an effort to block some of the reflection of the light behind her, to see if she could tell what was out there. Narrowing her eyes, she waited to see if the movement would come again.

"Oh, I'm sorry. I didn't realize there was someone here."

Lanie spun around quickly at the sound of the masculine voice, startled not only by the disruption to her solitary contentment, but also because she had genuinely forgotten she was in a public place full of people, any of whom could have wandered into the sunroom off the busy hallway beyond the door. *Startled* turned into *delighted,* however, when she realized who the masculine voice belonged to. Her eyes had adjusted to the darkness by now, and she had no trouble making out with—uh, she meant *making out*—Miles Fortune. Of all people. Well, well, well.

"That's okay," she said. "I was actually just getting ready to leave."

And why did she tell him that? she wondered. A handsome man she'd found fascinating for years shows up in a room where she'd have his undivided attention, and she tells him she has to be going? What was the matter with her?

"Don't let me scare you off," he said.

As if, Lanie thought. He was way too yummy to be scary. Most of the photos she'd seen of him had depicted him in casual clothes, everything from grubby ranch denim to preppy golf shirts and trousers to blazers with open-collar shirts and Dockers. Tonight, though, he'd dressed for the formal fund-raiser in a dark suit with a plum-colored dress shirt and a dappled silk necktie knotted at his throat.

Snazzy, she couldn't help thinking. Not a bad dresser for a guy who made his living chasing cows. She wondered if he had a woman stashed somewhere who helped him with his wardrobe. She'd read enough about Miles Fortune to know he never stayed with one woman for very long and, in fact, had dated some of the flashiest, most sophisticated women in Texas. But he had a sister and female cousins, and everyone knew those Fortunes were very close. Maybe one of his feminine relatives helped him make his sartorial selections.

Most men couldn't be bothered with that kind of thing. Especially those whose chief interests were bovine in nature.

Then again, part of Miles Fortune's appeal to all those flashy, sophisticated women was how great he looked all the time, Lanie reminded herself. So which was a result of the other? One of those chicken-or-the-egg things she'd probably be better off not thinking about, she supposed.

"You didn't scare me off," she said, remembering that he'd made a comment that had invited a reply.

He smiled in response, a smile that was sweet and dreamy and—there was just no escaping it—droolworthy. Lanie battled the temptation to swipe her hand over her mouth and smiled back.

"Good," he said. "Because the last thing I'd want to do is scare off a nice girl like you."

A nice girl, Lanie echoed to herself, turning fully around now to face him. Funny, she hadn't been called that for a long time. Maybe not ever. Whenever she was mentioned in the society pages or elsewhere, she was usually tagged with some cutesy nickname by whomever was doing the mentioning, and rarely were the nicknames in any way appropriate—or earned. Every time Lanie visited a new town, she was awarded some new, usually alliterative label she didn't deserve. The Dallas Delilah. The Houston Heartbreaker. The Fort Worth Firebrand. The San Antonio Seductress. The Amarillo Angel. The Corpus Christi Cutie. Or just the all-inclusive Texas Tornado. And then there was the one she had to suffer when she was at home in Austin: Government Goddess.

Oh, all right. So maybe she did kind of like that last one.

At any rate, "nice girl" had never been anywhere in the

mix. Not even when she'd gone to Nacogdoches. No, there she'd been The Knockout. So hearing Miles Fortune refer to her as a nice girl now made a little ripple of pleasure purl right through her.

"Hi, I'm Miles Fortune," he introduced himself. With a hint of self-consciousness—though whether real or manufactured to put her at ease, Lanie couldn't have said—he strode slowly across the room to where she stood, stopping when there was still a good three feet separating them, obviously not wanting her to feel threatened by him. Then, looking uncertain about how welcome the gesture would be, he extended his hand for her to shake it.

Lanie took it automatically, totally comfortable with the masculine form of address, because she'd been shaking the hands of her father's colleagues since she was a little girl. Something like that had always presented a great photo opportunity, after all. Besides, she didn't feel at all threatened by Miles Fortune, since he was in no way a threatening guy.

"I know who you are," she told him, still smiling warmly as she gave his hand a spirited shake.

He arched his dark eyebrows in surprise at the comment, even though Lanie was certain that what she had said couldn't possibly come as a surprise to him. "Then you have me at a disadvantage," he replied, still holding her hand, even though he'd stopped shaking it. "Because I don't know who you are."

It took a moment for the comment to register with Lanie, because she honestly didn't think anyone had ever said such a thing to her before. Invariably, people knew who she was: the governor's daughter. Even before her father had ascended to that lofty position, people had still known who

Lanie was. When the Meyerses had lived in Dallas, she'd been the mayor's daughter. Before that, in the third district, she'd been the alderman's daughter. Her father had held a political office of one kind or another since before she'd been born, and Lanie had always attended functions with him and her mother where she had been introduced as his daughter.

Which made her realize, perhaps for the first time, just how intrinsically her identity was linked to whatever position her father happened to hold. Her social life before turning eighteen had always been limited to functions that were also attended by her parents, something due largely to matters of security, she knew. Even before her father had climbed the higher rungs of the political ladder, he'd deliberately stayed visible in the public eye in order to reach those rungs, and he'd made sure his family was visible, too, because it made him more sympathetic.

Ironically, however, that public life had brought with it an essential need for privacy. Anyone who held public office might become a target for some lunatic. And, by extension, so might that person's family. So Tom and Luanne Meyers had made sure their young daughter was well protected at all times. That had meant keeping her *out* of public when they weren't with her, something that had rather limited Lanie's social life as an adolescent.

Lanie had never resented it, though. Well, not as much as she probably could or should have. She had just shrugged it off as a simple misfortune of birth. She had had benefits that a lot of teenage girls would never have, and that had provided her some compensation. Instead of a single bedroom, she'd had a suite of rooms at home. Her wardrobe had been full of party dresses and shoes for the appearances she made with her parents. She went to the salon twice a month to have her hair and nails done. She'd met the members of both *NSYNC and the Backstreet Boys when they'd played Dallas. And she'd visited movie sets and met television stars. For not having a social life, Lanie had been a big part of Texas society.

And she'd reassured herself by promising herself that she'd take advantage of adulthood once she turned eighteen, then strike out on her own and make her own impression on the world. But even over the past several years, when Lanie had been struggling to stand on her own two feet, she'd still never found herself in a situation where people didn't know who she was: the governor's daughter.

The realization didn't set well with her.

And maybe that was why she decided not to tell Miles Fortune her name. Well, not her full name. Because suddenly it was kind of nice not being recognized. Suddenly it was kind of nice not being the governor's daughter. Suddenly it was kind of nice just to be—

"Lanie," she said, noticing how she and Miles still hadn't released each other's hands. "I'm Lanie."

She could tell by his expression that he was waiting for her to give him her last name, too. And when she didn't, she could tell by his expression that he thought it was because she was a woman meeting a man for the first time and feeling cautious. He didn't press the matter, however. And something about that made her like him even more.

"Lanie," he said, smiling. "Pretty name."

And she could tell by his expression *that* time that her name wasn't the only thing he thought was pretty. But he didn't press that matter, either. And something about that made her like him even more, too.

"Thanks," she told him. "It's short for Elaine, which was my grandmother's name."

"It suits you," he said, still smiling, still not releasing her hand.

Not that Lanie minded.

But he didn't clarify which name suited her, she noted. That was interesting, because to her way of thinking, the two names had nothing in common, even though one was derived from the other. She'd always thought of Elaine as the name of an elegant, refined, cerebral brunette. Lanie was a party girl, plain and simple, laughing and dressed in bright colors and always the last to leave the dance floor. Lanie had always suited her much better, she'd always thought. Surely that was the one Miles was referring to, since he'd said it was pretty.

Still neither seemed in any hurry to release the other's hand, something Lanie decided not to worry too much about. Mostly because Miles's hand in hers just felt very, very nice, and it had been a long time since she'd held hands with a guy. The fact that she was doing so now for reasons that were in no way romantic was beside the point. Just looking at Miles Fortune made her feel romantic. Besides, this was only a brief little interlude that would be over all too quickly, and soon she'd only have memories of her chance meeting with Miles to keep her company. She wanted to make sure she had as many of them as she could to treasure. It wasn't every day a woman got to meet a Fortune, after all.

But as much as Lanie was enjoying herself at the moment, she knew better than to think that this momentary chance encounter would turn into anything more. For one thing, she wasn't such a lucky person that she ran into dreamy men like Miles Fortune every day. For another thing, the reason Miles Fortune was so dreamy was because that was where he dwelled—in Lanie's dreams. In reality, he wasn't the kind of man to let anything with a woman go much beyond the chance-encounter stage. And although Lanie Meyers might have the reputation for being a wild child, and although she might have a string of suggestive nicknames following her around Texas, when all was said and done, she really did know better than to get involved with a man like him. She liked to party. She didn't like getting her heart broken.

"So you had to escape the governor's bash, too, huh?" Miles asked now, referring to their earlier silent toast.

"Well, it was getting a bit crowded in there," she said.

Finally, finally, she made herself glance down at their still-joined hands, then back up at Miles with a meaningful look. He mimicked her actions, grinned and, with obvious reluctance, released her fingers. Lanie pulled her hand back unwillingly, but she figured it was silly for the two of them to stand there as if they'd been bonded with Superglue. People should know each other at least a little bit before epoxying themselves to each other. He buried the hand that had held hers in his trouser pocket, and lifted the other, holding a glass of amber-colored liquor to his mouth for a meager sip.

Lanie watched, fascinated, as he completed the gesture, noting everything she could about him in that brief, unguarded moment. How the bright moonlight filtering through the glass ceiling overhead glinted off of the heavy onyx ring on his third finger, flickered in the cut crystal of the glass and winked off the gold cuff link fixed in his shirt. She noticed, too, the confident way his fingers curled around the glass, the square, blunt-cut but well-kept fingernails, the dark hair on the back of his hand, making that part of him so different from that part of her. Her own hands were pale and slender, the nails expertly manicured and painted bright pink. Then her gaze traveled to his face, and she saw the scant shadow of day-old beard that darkened his angular jaw, the perfect, elegant slope of his aristocratic nose, the thick, black lashes that put her own heavily mascaraed ones to shame. As he lowered his glass, she remarked the beautifully formed mouth, how his lower lip was just a shade plumper than the upper one, giving him a sort of brooding look that was at odds with his laughing brown eyes.

She hadn't thought it would be possible for Miles Fortune to be even more handsome up close than he was from a distance. Most men who were that perfect-looking from afar became a bit less so when one drew nearer. Their eyes weren't quite as clear as first thought, or their mouths were a bit lopsided, or their complexions were marred by some kind of imperfection. But not Miles Fortune. Up close, the flawlessness of his good looks was only cemented more completely.

After lowering his glass, his gaze met Lanie's again, and he opened that beautiful mouth with the clear intention of saying something else. But he halted before uttering a word, his eyes widening when they met hers. And that was when Lanie realized her fascination with him must be written all over her face, and that she wasn't the only one who could tell what others were thinking by looking at them.

Which was *not* good, since what she was thinking about just then didn't bear airing anyplace other than in her own fantasies. Mostly because it involved Miles Fortune's face.

More specifically, it involved her *touching* Miles Fortune's face. And then moving on to other body parts.

Immediately she snapped her eyes closed and shook her head once, as if trying to physically dislodge her wayward thoughts. "Um," she began eloquently. "Ah," she added articulately. "Er," she then concluded astutely.

She heard Miles chuckle and opened her eyes to find him grinning at her again. But he was enough of a gentleman to pretend he hadn't just caught her mentally undressing him, or noticed the sudden lapse in her vocabulary. Which went beyond making her like him even more and pretty much ensured that she would be head over heels in love with him for the rest of her life.

Damn. That was going to be tough to explain to her future husband. Whoever the poor sap turned out to be.

"So what brought you to the governor's gig tonight?" Miles asked, thankfully changing the subject.

Then Lanie remembered they'd been talking about the governor's gig all along, and the only thing that had changed in the last few minutes had been her body temperature. "I came with my parents," she said, congratulating herself for having spoken the truth. "How about you?" she hurried to add, before he could ask her who her parents were.

"Dennis Stovall, the governor's campaign manager, is a friend of mine from college," Miles said. "I was in Austin on business this week and gave them a call the way I always do. They invited me to tag along tonight."

Right, Lanie thought, remembering her mother's earlier remark. She made a mental note of Miles's connection to Dennis and Jenny Stovall, thinking she might need it someday.

"So then you'll have to leave Austin soon," she surmised, "and go back to…"

Most of the Fortunes lived in Red Rock, Lanie knew. About twenty miles east of San Antonio, it hadn't become just another bedroom community and had instead held on to its own individual charm. Lanie had visited the town twice. First with her parents, when her father was stumping for his original attempt at the governor's mansion, eight years ago. He'd lost that election by a narrow margin, something that had only made him that much more determined to win next time around—which, of course, he had. But back when Lanie had visited Red Rock, she'd been a teenager, still enamored of the Fortune triplets, and more than a little excited to be visiting their home base. Mostly what she remembered from that brief visit was an enchanting little village, complete with town square—which was actually round, she remembered, but did claim the requisite white gazebo—and whose downtown claimed for focal features a café and a knitting shop.

Over the past five or six years, though, Red Rock had grown into a more bustling community, which Lanie had seen for herself when she'd gone there a second time last month as an emissary of her father to meet with Ryan Fortune with regard to his receiving the Hensley-Robinson Award. Its quaint Main Street had become a booming thoroughfare by then, one that included more upscale shops and restaurants. The café and knitting shop had still been thriving, though, so the town was maintaining its roots well.

Ryan Fortune's ranch, the Double Crown, had been a Fortune family stronghold for decades, and lay just outside of Red Rock. Not far from it was the Flying Aces, which Miles Fortune and his brothers had built several years ago.

Now, though, Steven Fortune lived near Austin. That was where her father's party for Ryan would take place next month. Lanie was already looking forward to it. Not just because it promised to be a very nice event, but because she'd bet good money Miles Fortune would be there, too, and it might provide her with another opportunity to run into him for another momentary chance encounter.

Well, it *might*.

All right, all right, so Lanie's fascination with the triplets hadn't ended when her adolescence had. Sue her. Maybe someday she'd get back to Red Rock again. After all, it wasn't that far from Austin. You never knew whom you might run into once you got there.

"Red Rock," he said now, answering the question she already knew the answer to. "It's near San Antonio. A small town. Making me a small-town guy. Pretty boring when you get right down to it."

Oh, Lanie wouldn't say that.

"Do you and your folks live here in Austin?" he asked.

"We do, actually," she replied without thinking. Not that Miles was going to make the leap that she was the governor's daughter by virtue of her living in Austin. Still, she didn't want to give him too many hints.

"Nice city," he said.

"It is," she agreed.

"Did you grow up here?"

She shook her head, content now to be making small talk. "I grew up in Texas," she said, "but I've lived in several different cities. Dallas, Fort Worth. I was born in Houston. And I spent a lot of my summers in Corpus Christi and Galveston."

He smiled. "You really are a Texas girl."

"How about you?" she asked, again already knowing the answer, but wanting to hear him speak it in that luscious, velvety baritone of his anyway.

"I actually grew up in New York City," he said. "But I spent summers here when I was a kid, and I just fell in love with the place. Couldn't wait to move out here permanently. Same for my brothers. The Fortunes have deep roots in Texas. Steven and Clyde and I wanted to put down roots right alongside them."

"That's right," Lanie said, feigning a vague recollection. "I think I remember reading about you Fortunes from time to time," she added in an oh-yeah-now-I-remember voice that she hoped masked her intense, youthful crush on him and his brothers. "You're one of the triplets, aren't you?"

He smiled this time in a way that let her know how genuinely delighted he was by being one of three—and which told her again which of the three he was, thanks to that yummy dimple. "Yeah, I am. But I have another, older, brother named Jack, and a younger sister, too. Violet."

"That must be interesting being a triplet. Identical, at that. I can't imagine another person in the world looking like me, let alone *two* other people in the world."

He shrugged, but continued to smile. "I've never known what it's like *not* to have two people in the world who look like me," he said. "Besides, Steven and Clyde and I are totally different personality-wise. I think it's kind of great, actually."

"I can see that," Lanie told him. "Five kids, though. That's a big family you come from."

"Don't you have brothers or sisters?" he asked. And something about the way he asked it made Lanie think he'd never even considered the possibility that there might be people in the world who didn't claim siblings at all.

She shook her head. "I'm an only child."

"Wow," he said, sounding impressed. "I can't imagine what that must be like. To never have anyone to play with or scuffle with or talk to when you need to confide in someone."

Lanie couldn't imagine why his comment put her on the defensive, but it did. "I had *lots* of people to play with growing up," she said, not quite able to mask the indignation that bubbled up inside her for some reason, and for which she was totally unprepared. "And I had *lots* of people to confide in. I was very, very popular at school and I was never, ever lonely."

Even she could see how obvious it was that she was protesting way too much. And okay, so maybe she was stretching the truth, she immediately conceded. Maybe the *lots* she had mentioned was really only… Well, zero.

And, anyway, she *had* had friends. A few. Just because she'd never felt all that close to any of them didn't mean anything.

"I'm sorry," he hastily apologized. "I didn't mean to imply that you were lonely. Or unpopular. Or anything like that."

"Good," Lanie said, still feeling a bit snippy, mostly because Miles Fortune had just struck a little too close to home, in spite of her protests to the contrary.

"Look, for what it's worth," he said, his voice softening some, "my family's got its share of dysfunctions, too."

"I never said my family was dysfunctional," Lanie said, the indignation returning. "Because we're not. We're totally normal," she assured him. "Totally, completely, utterly, absolutely normal."

If one considered being the first family of Texas normal. If one considered having a father with his eye on the White House normal. If one considered having lived in almost a half-dozen cities by the time one was ten years old normal. If one considered having buckets of money and unlimited social status normal.

So maybe the Meyerses weren't exactly normal. They certainly weren't dysfunctional. Well, no more than any normal family.

Now Miles laughed outright. "I didn't mean to imply that you'd been neglected and mistreated," he said. "I just meant—" He blew out an exasperated breath. "Ah, hell. I'm sorry, Lanie."

"You don't have to apologize," she said, letting go of her uneasiness. "I guess, really, my family isn't all that normal. But it's not a bad family."

"Neither is mine," he said. "There are just times when I wish they'd been more…" He shrugged, then smiled again. "Normal," he concluded.

"What do you mean?"

Belatedly, she realized what a personal, inappropriate question it was to ask him. The two of them had just met, after all, even if Lanie had known who Miles Fortune was for years. It was none of her business what the Fortune family dynamics were out of the public eye. Or even in the public eye, really. Unfortunately, thanks to reality television and infotainment shows, no one's life was really private anymore. Voyeurism had become a real spectator sport in this country. And Miles was the one who'd brought it up, she reminded herself. Not that that made it okay for Lanie to pry.

But he didn't seem offended by the question. On the contrary, he told her readily enough, "My parents were—and still are—very busy people, and sometimes they got stretched pretty thin. Don't get me wrong. We always knew how much they loved us, and family was more important to my folks than anything. But with five kids and being passionate about so many things, they needed more hours in the day. I just would have liked to have them around more. Does that make sense?"

Oh, it made perfect sense to Lanie. Not so much about the Fortunes. But she knew herself what it was like to have too-busy parents who weren't always around. It was hard to be resentful, though, because she knew they loved her, and what they were doing was to make her life better as much as their own. But it was hard to understand that when you were just a kid.

"Yeah, that makes sense," she said in response to Miles's question, not sure when she'd made the decision to speak aloud. "My folks are like that, too. They have important stuff to do. They're important people," she added.

"Same here," Miles said. "Good people, but busy people."

Lanie and Miles began to talk a lot after that, about so many things. Their childhoods, their schooling, their families. Things they hoped to do in the future, things they wished they had never done in the past. By the end of an hour together, they were seated at one of the tables in the corner of the sunroom as comfortably as if they were enjoying dinner at a restaurant. Miles had gone to the bar for another drink and returned with not only a glass of wine for Lanie, as well, but a book of matches to light the candle on the table so that the two of them would have some light.

Gradually, it occurred to Lanie that this was, without

question, the most enjoyable evening she'd ever spent anywhere, with anyone. Miles was just so easy to talk to, and something inside both of them connected in a way that felt easy, natural and right. She kept telling herself she needed to get back to the fund-raiser, that her parents would be looking for her. Then she'd remind herself that it was still early, that these things usually lasted till well past midnight and that she could spare a little more time to talk to Miles.

Unfortunately, just as Lanie was thinking that maybe she *wouldn't* go back to the fund-raiser ever again—or anywhere else where Miles Fortune wasn't—their conversation came to an abrupt halt. Because that was when the fern hanging immediately behind him and just above his head suddenly snapped free of its mooring, sending what looked like its entire contents raining down onto his head, his shoulders and into his jacket and shirt. In fact, she felt more than a little dirt splatter her own face and hair as it cascaded over Miles, skittering over her bare shoulders and working its way down the front of her dress.

For a moment, neither of them spoke, or moved, or blinked. They just sat there, frozen in the moon-kissed and candlelit darkness, their hands held up impotently to stop what had already finished happening. Or maybe they were surrendering to the inevitable, Lanie couldn't help thinking, whatever that inevitable might be. In any event, she suspected they both looked pretty foolish. Miles must have thought so, too, because in the next moment, as one, they both began to laugh. Hard.

Miles, gentleman that he was—however involuntarily in this case—took the worst of the hit, she saw. Where her own dress would probably be fine after a thorough shaking, his jacket and shirt might very well be goners. Little piles of soil perched on each of his shoulders like epaulets, and a veritable pyramid sat atop his head. Without thinking, he gave his hair a good shake, toppling the pyramid and sending a good bit of it down on Lanie. She gasped as she jumped up from her seat and took a few steps backward. Miles halted immediately, standing to help her. But that just sent more dirt flying.

"Oh, man, I am so sorry," he apologized. But he didn't quite manage to hide his grin. "I didn't mean to get you even dirtier."

Instead of being offended, Lanie began to laugh again. "I don't know that it's possible for either one of us to get dirtier at this point," she told him. She looked at the offending planter, still swinging haphazardly behind him. "How on earth did that happen?"

He turned around, too, to inspect the culprit, and Lanie was surprised to see it hadn't quite emptied, since there was still dirt trickling out of it. The poor fern, though, was a definite casualty, lying in a heap on the floor behind him.

"I have no idea," he said when he turned back around. "Must have had a loose link in the chain or something." He shook his arms this time, less vigorously than he had his head, and dirt tumbled off of him quite liberally.

"I guess we should be grateful they hadn't watered the plants for a while," she said, fighting another fit of giggles. "Otherwise it might have been a mudslide. I hope you didn't pay a lot for that jacket."

"It wasn't the jacket that was expensive," he said.

"No?"

He shook his head slowly in response...something that just made more dirt fall to his shoulders and into the garment in question. "No, it was the whole suit," he said.

Thankfully, he didn't specify a price, but Lanie, who had an excellent eye for fashion, figured it had been at least four figures.

"What about you?" he said, jutting his chin up in the direction of her person. "Are you going to be able to salvage that dress?"

She shrugged…and felt the dirt in her bodice shift into her bra. Okay, so maybe she'd taken a worse hit than she'd thought. "What, this old thing?" she asked with a smile, even though she'd only worn the dress once before. "I dust with this."

He laughed outright at that and began brushing half-heartedly at his shirt again. "We can't go back into the party like this," he said. "Not only do we look a mess, but people will wonder what the hell we've been up to all this time. It won't look good."

"And people do tend to gossip a lot after an event like this," Lanie concurred wearily. She, too, began to brush at her clothing again, but really, when all was said and done, she wasn't *that* big a mess. Miles had far more to worry about than she did.

"Give me your jacket," she said. "I'll try to shake out as much as I can. Maybe if you free your shirttail, you can get most of the dirt out of your shirt."

"That's okay," he said. "I can manage. I'm sorry. I didn't mean to get you all dirty, too. You go on back. There's a ladies' room before you get back to the ballroom. You can get yourself cleaned up in there."

"Not until we've gotten you cleaned up in here," Lanie objected. "Come on. There's no one around. Give me your jacket and shake out your shirt. It will only take a minute."

With clear reluctance, he shrugged out of his jacket and

handed it to her. She turned away from him as he began to untuck his shirt, in an effort to give him a little privacy, regardless of how innocent the action was. Holding his jacket out at arm's length, she gave it a gentle shake, but that one movement freed a considerable cloud of dirt, so she turned the jacket upside down, releasing handfuls of dirt from the pockets. She scooped her hand inside each one to free as much of the leftover soil as she could. Then, spreading the jacket open wide in front of her, she started to give it another shake…

Only to be blinded by a flash of glaring white light from the other side of the window in front of her.

Three

No, it wasn't just one flash of light, Lanie realized as she blinked against the dizzying display, but dozens of them, one right after the other. Flash, flash, flash, flash, flash. Then a brief pause. Then another round. The flashes were so bright, and so fast, and there were so many of them, that Lanie instinctively closed her eyes and pulled Miles's jacket up over her face to block them.

She wasn't sure what happened after that. She heard Miles utter a few choice oaths and epithets behind her; then he dashed between her and the window to block her from view of whatever was on the other side. She started to lower his jacket, but he stayed her hands and jerked the garment back up in front of her again, preventing her from seeing what was going on.

"Don't," he told her in a voice edged with something vicious and dangerous. "Keep your face covered."

"What's happening?" Lanie asked, completely befuddled now.

Instead of receiving an answer from him, she felt him wrap an arm around her shoulders, his other hand holding the jacket in a way that allowed her to see where she was going but kept her face hidden. He hurried her out of the sunroom, but instead of turning left, to go back to the party—and a crowd of people—he turned right and hurried them both in that direction. Lanie let him do it, figuring he knew more about what was going on than she did, since he'd seized control of the situation so quickly and expertly. They didn't slow down until Miles was leading them down a narrow corridor, and she could see just well enough through the slightly parted lapels of his jacket to know he was leading her to a men's restroom.

For the first time that evening, she felt real fear.

But she immediately tamped it down. Whatever his reason was for leading her this way, it had to be a good one, she told herself. He didn't mean her any harm. Even though she still didn't know what the hell was going on, she felt absolutely certain that Miles Fortune was no threat to her. They'd passed a perfectly nice evening in conversation and had shared some pretty intimate parts of themselves with each other during that time. They'd laughed together. Hoped together. Dreamed together. They'd made each other feel good. Miles was a nice man. Period. Hey, maybe he didn't even realize he was leading her into a men's room.

So she told him, "I can't go in there." She dug her feet into the lush pile of the carpeting. "That's the men's room."

He muttered something unintelligible under his breath and released her. "Wait here, then," he said softly, pushing past her to enter first.

Although Lanie told herself she must be seeing things, that her skewed view from beneath the jacket was playing tricks on her vision, she could have sworn Miles wasn't wearing a shirt when he entered.

Nah, she told herself immediately. Couldn't be.

But in a matter of seconds, the men's room door was swinging open again, and there stood Miles in front of her. Sure enough, his chest was as bare as the day he was born, and his shirt was clutched in one hand.

What the…? she thought.

"What the…?" she began to speak her thoughts aloud.

But Miles didn't give her the chance. "It's empty," he told her. Then he grabbed her hand and tugged hard, pulling her into the men's room behind him, whether she liked it or not.

And Lanie didn't.

Strangely, however, it wasn't because she felt any fear about the situation. No, it was because the moment she'd seen Miles bare-chested, she hadn't been able to push her brain any further forward. Not even the confusion and chaos of whatever the hell was going on bothered her anymore. The only thing that bothered her then was that Miles was half-naked and she wasn't.

She hated it when that happened.

He was magnificent, she thought. Splendidly formed, his torso and shoulders and arms were solid and muscular without being overblown. Some of that was no doubt due simply to the physical labor of ranch work, as was the burnished bronze of his skin that lingered even now, in November. But he'd taken care with his abs, too, no mistaking that, because each and every one was exquisitely outlined. A dark, rich scattering of hair winged its way from one brawny shoulder to the other, spiraling down to disappear into what Lanie now saw was an unfastened belt and button on his trousers.

Just what the hell was going on?

"Just what the hell is going on?" she demanded, once again speaking her thoughts out loud, only this time having the presence of mind to complete them. She jerked his jacket off and tossed it at him, heedless of how the gesture sent strands of blond hair flying around her face. Pushing them haphazardly out of her eyes, she further demanded, "Why are you undressed? Why did you throw your jacket over my head? What was on the other side of the window, making that flash—"

And then, like a poorly potted fern, it hit her. She realized what had happened. She understood because it had happened to her before. She'd just been too caught up in falling head over heels for Miles Fortune to figure it out before now.

A photographer. She'd been the subject of enough photo opportunities with her father to recognize the rapidity and white light of the flashes. And not just from her father's campaign, either, but because she was often followed by photographers herself when she visited new places. She was a regular feature in the society pages, after all, however evenhandedly she was portrayed—which was usually not evenhandedly at all. The fallout from tonight, she was certain, would be no exception.

Oh, no, she thought, dread filling her stomach. Tonight. Tonight, she'd been ambushed worse than ever before. She and Miles both. They'd been together, alone, in the sunroom. And they'd been...

Oh, no.

She looked at his bare chest and unfastened pants again, unable to look at anything else. Miles must have noticed her scrutiny, because he hastily shrugged back into his shirt and even more hastily began to button it. But he missed one somewhere along the way and had to start over again. And Lanie could have no more averted her gaze from him then than she could have stopped the sun from rising in the morning.

For a moment, she forgot all about the fact that she'd just been photographed in a compromising position with Miles Fortune. Because the only thing filling her brain was how he looked dressing and undressing and dressing again, and how it might be if his reasons for doing so were different.

Get a grip, Lanie, she told herself. *This is serious. Stop drooling.*

"What the hell happened?" Miles echoed her question of a moment ago. "I'll tell you what the hell happened. What the hell happened is that you and I were just photographed by Nelson Kaminski, one of the vilest, scummiest, son-of-a-bitch photographers in the paparazzi, that's what. And ever since I had him busted for harassment, he's made it his life's work to make my life hell."

Lanie nodded, not because she recognized the name of the photographer, but because she understood the tactics of the paparazzi. Nothing was sacred to them. They were a breed unto themselves, completely set apart from the legitimate photojournalists she'd met during her father's political career-building. Those guys waited for planned photo ops to snap pictures, or, at the very least, waited until she or a member of her family was at a public gathering in a public place. And for the most part, they did a fairly decent job of accurately portraying the situation.

Guys like this Nelson Kaminski, on the other hand, went out of their way to ambush their subjects at the most inopportune or inappropriate moments, and they did their best to make their photos as sensational as possible. If they couldn't find a situation that was legitimately sensational, then they altered their photos—and even the situation—to create the sensation themselves.

Lanie looked at Miles again, watching as he fastened the last button and began to stuff his shirttail back into his pants. "What were you doing with your shirt off?" she asked halfheartedly, even though she pretty much knew the answer.

He glanced up from what he was doing and met her gaze, his eyes full of an apology he really wasn't obligated to give. "You had your back turned," he said. "Shaking out my jacket. I turned around, too, thought I could just shake out my shirt in a couple seconds and put it back on before you even noticed. My trousers…" He inhaled deeply and exhaled the breath in a long, exasperated sigh. "Well, I was just trying to work quickly, you know? I never thought you'd see me. And if you did, well… I thought the position was innocent enough. I had my back turned to you," he said again. Then, more softly, he added, "Until the first flash went off. That's when I turned around, still half-dressed. And that was when the flashes really started popping."

He shrugged, looking tired and defeated. "When I said I didn't mean to get you dirty earlier, Lanie, this wasn't what I was talking about. Unfortunately, I think I just got you dirtier than you ever thought you could get. Thanks to your association with me, you've just become fodder for the tabloids. Tomorrow morning, you might just wake up and find yourself under a headline that says something

about you being a mystery woman who's the latest acqui-
sition of Miles Fortune."

Lanie appreciated his effort to take responsibility for
what had happened, and under other circumstances she
might have let him. Because under other circumstances,
Miles Fortune would have been the target of the photographer. But not this time, she was sure. Not when there
were less than two weeks left before the election. Not
when she'd heard so many lectures from her father about
how important it was for her to maintain some semblance
of propriety, now more than ever, because anything she said
or did in public might be misconstrued and used against
him. As much as she wished she could be a mystery woman
right now, she knew it just wasn't realistic—or likely.

"I don't think it was you the photographer was after tonight," she told Miles softly. "At least, he wasn't after you
alone."

Miles narrowed his eyes at her in clear puzzlement.
"What do you mean?"

She smiled weakly. "You really don't know who I am,
do you?" she asked.

"I know enough," he said. "I know you're Lanie, and
that you're nice, and that you're sweet, and that you're
easy to talk to, and that you make me smile, and that you're
surprisingly comfortable to be with. What else do I need
to know?"

Now her smiled turned sad. "Well, there's my last name,
for starters."

"What difference does your last name make?"

"Normally, it wouldn't make any difference at all. But
in this case, Miles, it makes a huge difference. Because my
last name is Meyers. I'm Lanie Meyers." She could tell by

his expression that he understood then. That the two names put together told him everything he needed to know. Nevertheless, she continued, "My father is Tom Meyers, the governor of Texas."

To herself, she added silently, *But after this, he may not be governor for long....*

Miles studied Lanie for several moments in silence. The governor's daughter. He realized now he probably should have recognized her right off the bat, but who paid attention to such things? Whenever he'd seen the first family of Texas on TV, he'd been listening to what the governor was saying, not ogling the man's daughter. And Miles had better things to do than read the parts of the newspaper that only talked about who went to what parties with whom, and what designers' fashions they were wearing when they did. And that was where Lanie Meyers was whenever she made the news. Which was fairly often. Miles did know that. He'd heard his sister and cousins talk about the girl from time to time, and he supposed he'd absorbed some of the stories through osmosis. Still, she'd seemed harmless enough. A party girl. Not really unexpected when your daddy was a big-time politician.

But she hadn't seemed like a party girl tonight. Well, maybe at first she had, he amended. But after just five minutes alone with her, Miles knew she was a lot more than that. Lanie Meyers was a nice girl who was witty and funny and easy to talk to. And she was maybe a little bit lonely, too. And that last had been what had ultimately cemented Miles's connection to her, because he'd recognized in Lanie so much of what was inside himself.

How about that? You really couldn't believe everything you read in the papers.

He grimaced involuntarily as he thought about what kind of stories would be appearing about Lanie in the papers over the next several days. Although they wouldn't be true, that didn't mean people wouldn't lap up every last word as the gospel truth and talk about it at the office water cooler. Or the backyard clothesline. Or the grocery counter. Or the tennis nets. Or wherever else they happened to be.

Lanie Meyers. Miles Fortune had just been photographed in what could easily be misconstrued as a compromising position with the governor's daughter. Had the situation not been so unfair, it would have been funny.

He supposed he should have expected something like this would happen sooner or later. If not with that bastard Kaminski, then with another slimy photographer. Miles Fortune was something of a hothead when it came to having his photo taken. As a result, he'd become a real challenge for the members of the local paparazzi. It wasn't that he was especially famous or notorious. But he *did* hate to have his photo in the paper, and he'd reacted badly on occasion in the past.

Truthfully, though, it wasn't as much because Miles valued his privacy as it was because he didn't want the women he was escorting at any given time to be portrayed in a less-than-stellar light. And because he tended not to stay in relationships for very long—because he was a *womanizer,* he acknowledged with some distaste—the papers always intimated that the women he dated were little more than warm bodies to keep him entertained through the night.

Truthfully, Miles thought they were, too, for the most part. But that didn't make it okay for the press to cast the women in a bad light. His endless parade of girlfriends couldn't help it if each thought she'd be the one to make him change his ways and settle down. He just wasn't the settling-down type. They couldn't help it if they looked all besotted with him every time they showed up in a photo standing next to him. Hey, he was a very likable guy. That didn't mean the press had to hang those women out to dry the way they invariably did.

Now Lanie Meyers was going to be portrayed as little more than another notch on his bedpost. That was going to cast her in a much darker light than party girl, and it would inevitably reflect badly on her father and, as a result, on her father's campaign.

"Lanie Meyers," Miles repeated slowly, carefully, his head still too full of repercussions and implications to say much else.

She nodded as slowly and carefully as he had spoken. "Lanie Meyers," she confirmed.

"Governor Meyers's daughter," Miles echoed.

"Governor Meyers's daughter," she likewise confirmed.

"Bad dream?" he asked, hoping she'd confirm that, too.

She smiled, albeit not entirely happily. "Reality," she assured him.

He lifted one shoulder and let it drop. "Hey, it was worth a shot."

"So who's going to end up being most embarrassed by this?" she asked.

Hell, Miles didn't even have to think about that. And he was pretty sure it was a hypothetical question anyway. "Well, I imagine it'll be your old man."

"No imagining about it," Lanie told him. "It will definitely be my father. This is going to make him look incredibly bad."

It was an interesting comment on a number of levels, Miles thought, not the least of which was that at a time when Lanie should be worried more about herself and her own reputation than anyone else's, she was concerned only about her father's. She had yet to utter one word of concern for herself.

"But nothing happened," Miles pointed out, knowing how ridiculous it was to even say such a thing when Nelson Kaminski was anywhere in the same time zone.

"No, it didn't," she agreed. "But you and I both have had enough experience with the press to know that that's beside the point."

Miles nodded disconsolately. There was nothing either of them could do now but hope for the best. But he couldn't seem to let it go. Sighing with much exasperation, he added, "If I hadn't had my shirt off, we probably could have salvaged this."

"If you hadn't had your shirt off, there never would have been any photographs," Lanie pointed out. But there was no censure in her voice, no bitterness or resentment.

"Don't be so sure," Miles said, nevertheless. "Kaminski sniffed a potential photo the minute he saw us through the glass. Hell, for all I know, he'd gotten bored at the party because nothing scandalous enough was happening and went on the prowl specifically to find—or manufacture— a situation. Who knows how long he was out there lurking in the bushes? He was just waiting for one of us to do something that he could make look bad. Hell, you could have picked a loose thread off of my lapel, and he would have snapped a shot and worked with it until it looked like the two of us were groping each other."

"You sound like you're speaking from experience," Lanie said.

"Unfortunately I am," Miles told her. "But even knowing what I do about him, I still can't believe how low the guy will sink." He'd used a lot of restraint by calling the photographer a *guy* instead of a more accurate description. There was a lady present, after all. "Do you know," he continued, "that he actually developed and patented a way to use a camera flash so that it doesn't reflect off of glass? You know why? So he could take pictures of people through windows, like tonight. That's his specialty. And as long as he takes the pictures in a public place like this, there's nothing anyone can do about it. Unless he's skulking around bedroom windows, he's free and clear to prey on whoever he wants to."

That was exactly what Kaminski was, he thought. A predator. The kind of lowlife that just slithered around in the dark waiting for an opportunity. He could have crouched out there till sunup waiting for Lanie and Miles to do something indiscreet. And when they had done nothing indiscreet, Kaminski had jumped on a perfectly innocent episode to turn it into something tawdry.

That was exactly what that son of a bitch would do, Miles knew. He might be too late to make tomorrow's papers, but the day after, Miles and Lanie were going to be in every rag in Texas. And Kaminski would make damned sure it wasn't their best side showing.

"I feel responsible," he told Lanie now. "That guy's had it in for me for a long time. I had him busted after he photographed me with a woman who—"

There Miles stopped, because he wasn't sure how to say the rest. The woman he'd been with at the time was married, but he hadn't been seeing her romantically. In fact, she'd been seeking his advice because her husband was one of Miles's close friends. They'd met at a restaurant outside of Dallas, off the beaten path, not knowing that a rising Hollywood starlet who was in town filming a movie was also having dinner there. Kaminski had gone to the place hoping for a shot of her, but when he'd seen a member of the Fortune family, he'd figured he might as well make a couple extra bucks off of Miles, too.

He'd waited until an especially emotional outburst from the woman had caused Miles to reach across the table and touch her shoulder, then had snapped the shot and made it look as if Miles had been making a play for his best friend's wife. When her husband saw the photo in the paper two days later, the marriage she had been trying so hard to save was well and truly over.

"Let's just say he photographed me with someone he shouldn't have, in a situation he shouldn't have, and I made him regret it. Big-time."

First by punching the guy in the nose in the hope that he could snatch the camera out of Kaminski's hand. But when Kaminski had scuttled off like the cockroach he was and sold the photo to the highest bidder, Miles had turned to legal avenues. It hadn't saved the woman's marriage but ultimately, Miles had settled out of court for a tidy financial sum from Kaminski and the paper that had printed the photograph, money he'd turned around and donated to a local charity.

"Ever since then, the guy's been gunning for me," he told Lanie. "I can make him regret this, too," he added, "but not fast enough to keep those pictures out of the papers. I'm sorry," he said again, even though he knew the apology was cold comfort.

"How bad could it be?" she said, obviously trying to inject a cheerfulness into her voice that she didn't feel. "I mean, we weren't doing anything. Yeah, you had your shirt off, but we weren't standing close to each other. We weren't even facing each other. We'll just explain what happened and have a good laugh over it. And who knows? Maybe the pictures will be so innocent, there won't be anything for Kaminski to sell to anyone. This could all wind up being one huge nonevent."

Miles wished he could believe that was true. But he knew Kaminski. And he knew the American public. Kaminski would do his best to make Miles and Lanie look their worst. And the public would eat it up with a spoon, because everyone loved scandal. Especially a sex scandal. Especially a *political* sex scandal. Especially close to an election. Even if Lanie's father wasn't involved, the publicity could do damage to what Miles recalled now was a narrow lead in the polls.

"I hope you're right," he told Lanie, feeling a cold lump settle in the pit of his stomach. "I really hope you're right."

"Just wait," she said, smiling again, a smile that was so unbelievably hopeful Miles wanted to put an arm around her and pull her close. "Everything will be just fine," she said brightly. Too brightly. "Probably, no one will even see the photos, because they'll be buried on page nine of the society section, and they'll just look like two people who had a little too much to drink at a party. God knows, it won't be the first time a paper has said I was overly intoxicated. In spite of the fact that I never drink anything but club soda at public parties."

Miles wished he could share her conviction. But deep down inside, he had a very bad feeling about this.

Four

Governor Tom Meyers leaned back in the big, gubernatorial chair behind the big, gubernatorial desk in his big, gubernatorial office at the big, gubernatorial mansion in the not-so-big—but still gubernatorial—city of Austin and sighed with much satisfaction. The new polls had come out yesterday morning, and he was still ahead. Not by much, maybe, but he was still there, firmly entrenched in the hearts and minds of most Texans. Unless something went very wrong, the office was his for a second term.

He loved being governor of Texas. He loved being numero uno in the biggest, baddest, most kick-ass state in the union. Yeah, people said Alaska was really bigger, and, geographically speaking, he supposed that was true. But Alaska wasn't near as seasoned as Texas was. It didn't have the population, the big cities, the history, the character, the reputation.

And it sure as hell didn't send governors to the White House.

Yeah, the White House. That was Tom Meyers's ultimate destination. Someday he would be president of the United States of America. Nothing was going to stand in his way. He'd win this election, and then he'd run for national office. Maybe senator. Hell, maybe even president. Depended on how his second term went. But he knew the party had its eye on him, and he knew he was performing exactly the way it wanted him to. And once he won a second term, he would be well and truly on his way.

He ran a hand through the thick white hair he was so proud of. Once, it had been pale blond. But by the time he'd turned fifty, it had gone snow-white. He liked it, though. Thought it made him look more statesmanlike. Gave him an air of seniority and authority that age hadn't managed to endow just yet.

Flipping open the lid of the humidor that sat on his desk, he withdrew a fine Panamanian cigar. He would have preferred Cuban, but with the embargo still on, he didn't dare. He didn't want to do anything un-American, after all. If the media got ahold of even that small indiscretion, they'd play it up for all it was worth as the worst kind of conduct. Hell, he wouldn't be the first politician to be brought down by a cigar.

Besides, one of the reasons Tom arrived at the office so much earlier than the start of the regular workday was so that he could enjoy a few uninterrupted moments to ease into the day, smoking a good cigar, reading the newspaper, preparing himself for the day ahead before the phone started ringing off the hook and people started demanding so much of his time.

He had clipped off the end of the cigar and tucked it between his lips, and was reaching for the alabaster lighter next to the humidor when his office door flew open and his secretary bolted through it without so much as a by-your-leave. Tom opened his mouth to demand an explanation for the intrusion, but the look on Millie's face stopped him cold. Whatever was wrong, it was *very* wrong. The kind of wrong that could cost a man a narrow lead in the polls.

"Millie," he said in a cautious voice. "What is it?"

She said nothing in reply, only stood framed by the doorway for a moment, looking like a deer in the headlights. Her tan suit was the color of a big buck, her fawn-colored hair was tucked into a tidy bun at the back of her head and her brown eyes were wide with fear.

"Millie?" Tom tried a second time. "Is there a reason why you bolted into my office without so much as knocking?"

The question seemed to finally jar her from whatever stupor she'd fallen into, but she didn't apologize for the intrusion, which, under normal circumstances, she would have. Instead, she strode woodenly across the office and halted in front of Tom's desk. His gaze traveled from her troubled eyes to the folded newspaper she carried in one hand. It shouldn't have alarmed him. Millie always came into work early, too, and she always picked up a newspaper for him on her way in. Her appearance wouldn't have been alarming, had it not been for the look on her face that assured him something was very wrong.

"Millie," he said for a third time, in the same cautious voice. This time, though, he couldn't find it within himself to say anything more.

Millie didn't seem to need any additional prodding,

though. As she silently unfolded the newspaper and held it up for Tom to see, a billow of fiery dread went howling through his belly.

Lanie had pulled a lot of stunts in her short life. But this... This was beyond the pale.

Because there, on the front page of the *National Interrogator,* the country's sleaziest, most shameless, most notorious scandal sheet, was Governor Tom Meyers's daughter, Lanie.

Naked.

With a man.

Whom Tom recognized as being one of the biggest womanizers in Texas.

Not to mention a member of the opposing party.

Yep, that just about covered it. That pretty much put Lanie in a position that was utterly and completely indefensible. Even the greatest spin doctors in the world wouldn't be able to cast a positive light on this. Forget the White House. He'd be lucky to get a job at the International House of Pancakes after this.

"It's not the only one," Millie said. "But it's probably the worst."

"Probably?" Tom repeated.

Millie dropped her gaze to the floor. "Well, they're all pretty bad," she told him. "It was kind of hard to choose an absolute worst."

"How many are there?"

"Dozens," Millie replied, though she still didn't look at him. "From several different angles. And they've been picked up by every newspaper in the state, and more than a few nationally." She did glance up at Tom, for just a second, then dropped her gaze back to the floor. "They've been on all the morning shows, too," she told him. "Both local *and* national."

Tom closed his eyes and counted slowly to ten. Then to twenty. Then fifty. Then seventy-five. Then higher. Finally, somewhere around two hundred and eighty-seven, he calmed down enough to open his eyes again. Unfortunately, Millie hadn't moved an inch, and the photo of Lanie and Miles Fortune was still there in living color, mocking the death of Tom Meyers's career. Because Miles Fortune was still shirtless, with his pants unfastened.

And Lanie was still naked.

Oh, all the inappropriate parts of her body were covered by a man's jacket—not that that helped matters much, since it was pretty clear she'd just taken the jacket off of Fortune—but she was definitely naked on the other side of it. Her shoulders were bare above it, and her legs were bare beneath it, and with Miles standing the way he was, it looked as if the two of them had just finished a quickie coupling, from a position that Tom was pretty sure was still illegal in at least a dozen states—his own included.

This really wasn't good for a man who'd done a large part of his campaigning on the family values platform. And neither was the language he was of a mind to use at the moment. So instead of speaking, he reached for the newspaper and unfolded it completely, flattening it onto his desk.

Government Goddess Gets Good Fortune! screamed the headlines.

What the hell kind of headline was that for a newspaper to use? Tom asked himself, mostly because he didn't want to have to answer the million other questions ricocheting around his head at that moment.

"Even the *Dallas Tribune* published it," Millie told him.

The most conservative paper in the state, Tom thought. One that had endorsed him for office from day one. In the name of selling more papers, they'd sold him out.

"Millie," he said, amazed at how well he was able to keep his voice quiet and steady, "where is my daughter today?"

"As far as I know, she's at home, Governor," Millie told him. "I don't think she has anything scheduled until the end of the week. Oh, no, in two days," she corrected herself. "On Wednesday, she's supposed to accompany Mrs. Meyers on a trip to the children's hospital."

Oh, like anyone was going to let her get within fifty feet of children after this, Tom thought.

"And Miles Fortune?" the governor asked. "Is he still in town?"

Millie nodded. "Dennis Stovall mentioned that he and Jenny were having dinner with Mr. Fortune last night, so he must still be in town this morning."

Tom nodded once. "First, I want you to call Lanie at home. You call her right quick, and you tell her I want to see her."

"Yes, sir."

"You tell her she's not to say a word to anyone, anywhere, under any circumstances until after she's spoken to me."

"Yes, sir."

"You tell her to be here in my office in two hours."

"Yes, sir."

Tom inhaled deeply, held the breath inside until his rapid-fire heart rate slowed some, then exhaled in a slow, laborious breath. "And then, Millie, I want you to call Dennis and find out where Miles Fortune is staying, and I want you to get him on the phone."

"Yes, sir."

"And you tell him exactly what you told Lanie. Not to say a word to anyone about this until I speak to him, and to meet me here at the office right away."

"But, sir."

Tom wasn't used to hearing "buts" from Millie. So that one rather caught his attention. "Yes, Millie?"

She looked uncomfortable at having used the interjection, too. "Well, it's just that he's…" She lifted one shoulder and let it drop. "Miles Fortune," she said simply, as if that explained everything.

"So?"

"So you know those Fortunes," Millie said, regrouping some. "I mean, it's one thing to tell Lanie what to do—she's your daughter, and she'll do anything you say. But Miles Fortune? For all we know, he's out there passing out cigars over this."

Tom looked at the picture again, at the dark-haired, shirtless man standing behind his daughter. Miles Fortune looked in no way happy in that photo. No, he looked like a man as angry about and embarrassed by the photos being taken as Tom was.

The governor shook his head. "He's not passing out cigars," he said with finality.

"Well, he may not jump when you tell him to," Millie said. "He may want to deal with this in his own way."

Tom Meyers smiled, but there was no happiness in the gesture. "Oh, I don't think so, Millie," he said. "You tell Miles Fortune I want to see him immediately. And you tell him—" He hesitated a moment. "On second thought, Millie, let me call Fortune. I'll deal with him myself."

Instead of turning around and leaving to follow his orders, Millie stood in place, clearly having something else on her mind that she needed to say.

"Was there something else?" Tom asked her.

She shifted her weight from one foot to the other, clearly not liking what she was about to say. "Well…what about the reporters?" she finally asked.

Tom tensed, even though he knew her question was one he was going to have to consider soon. "When they call, just tell them no comment," he said. That was, after all, standard operating procedure.

"No," she said, growing more agitated. "I mean the reporters outside."

Great, Tom thought. Now he was going to have to sneak out of the capitol building somehow to avoid those guys all day. "Well, try to create a diversion while I use a side exit or something," he told Millie. "Besides, I won't be leaving for a while yet."

Millie shook her head. "No, I don't mean the reporters outside—though there are plenty out there, too. I mean the ones in the hallway," she told him. "The ones right outside the outer office. They're not going anywhere until they talk to you, Governor. You better think of something to say about this. Quick."

On any normal day, Miles would have no idea why he had been summoned to the office of the governor of Texas by none other than the man himself. But today was no ordinary day. No, today was the day that Miles had awakened to the ringing of the telephone before the hotel alarm clock had even had a chance to go off. Whenever he traveled, be it personal or for business, he seized every opportunity he had to sleep late. Since his flight back to San Antonio didn't leave until after noon, this morning was supposed to have provided such an opportunity. He'd have a lot of work for the rest of the week, to catch up on what he'd missed while out of town, and he figured he deserved to have an extra day to just relax.

But judging by the expression on the governor's face, he was pretty sure he wasn't going to be doing much relaxing for a long time.

"Do you know why you're here?" Tom Meyers asked him without preamble the moment he opened the door to his office.

Miles expelled a restless breath and said, "I imagine it has something to do with the morning papers."

After all, Miles had seen the paper himself before the sun had fully risen. A 5:00 a.m. phone call had awakened him. Ironically, it hadn't been the governor calling—no, that call had come later. It had been Miles's sister Violet, calling to ask him about the photographs that kept airing over and over again on the early-morning shows.

In spite of what he'd told Lanie about it probably taking a couple of days, Miles still marveled at how quickly the photos of the two of them had made it into print. Newspapers only rushed things to press for very important news stories. And even though Miles couldn't for the life of him figure out what could be newsworthy about two people spilling dirt on themselves, he knew the dirt on him and the governor's daughter was pretty thick. What was really funny was that the situation everyone thought was so dirty had actually been one of the cleanest episodes he'd ever shared with a woman.

"Come in," the governor said, taking a few steps backward to allow Miles entry.

He was dressed in a suit and tie, despite the early morning hour, and Miles guessed it was because there was a press conference in the man's near future. As soon as he stepped through the door, Tom Meyers closed it, then paced restlessly to the other side of the luxuriously appointed room and back again.

"Thank you for coming as I asked," he said as he made the journey. But there wasn't an ounce of gratitude or appreciation or anything else polite in the man's voice. On the contrary, the thank-you sounded as if it had been pulled from him painfully. And as for the "asked" part…

Asked? Miles echoed to himself. More like demanded. Before Miles had even been able to finish saying "hello" to that particular call, a man's voice had been bellowing at him about elections and lewd behavior and public intoxication and a daughter. That last had been what finally made Miles understand who was yelling at him and why. And when he'd realized he was being berated by the governor, he'd had no choice but to listen. Even if half of what the guy had said was incoherent.

The governor had gone on for a good five minutes before taking enough of a breath to allow Miles to say something. Unfortunately, Miles realized pretty quickly that he himself had no idea what to say. Which actually turned out to not be a problem, since the governor, once he completed his breath, let loose with both barrels again.

The gist of it had been that if Miles valued his social standing, his citizenship, his ranch, his Social Security benefits and his manhood, he'd report to the governor's office within the hour. So Miles had yanked on a pair of wrinkled blue jeans lying in a heap on the floor, had jerked a wadded-up denim work shirt off a chair, had stuffed his feet, sans socks, into a pair of boots and had thrown on a shearling jacket on his way out the door. And he'd made it to the governor's office with thirteen minutes to spare.

Now here he stood, watching the governor pace like a Chihuahua who'd consumed a bad batch of five-alarm chili, and listening to a harangue that wasn't a whole lot different from the one Miles had already suffered over the phone. Except that now, the term *election* seemed to be cropping up in every third sentence instead of every fifth, as it had earlier.

"That girl is going to be the death of me yet," the governor was saying now. "She's done some pretty stupid things in her life, but this takes the cake. It could very well cost me the election."

Yep, there it was again.

"Sir," Miles tried to interject, knowing that Lanie had done nothing wrong and that he couldn't let her take responsibility for what had happened, "if you'll just let me ex—"

But as he had done ever since Miles had entered the office poised to explain, the governor ignored him. "I love that girl, and she's been a bright spot in Luanne's and my life, but there are times when she just doesn't think. Lanie needs discipline, that's what she needs. And that's why she keeps getting into fixes like this."

"Sir," Miles tried again.

"And now her actions are going to hurt other people, too," the governor continued, heedless of Miles's interjection. "All the people who worked so hard on this campaign. Her mother. Me. This really could cost me a second term. Of all the thoughtless, selfish…"

Miles's jaw went rigid at that. For one thing, after an evening-long conversation with Lanie Meyers, he knew she wasn't selfish or thoughtless. If anyone in the Meyers family came across like that, it was Tom Meyers himself at the moment. Lanie's name was the one being dragged through the mud in the morning papers. Sure, Miles could see how that was going to affect her father's campaign—he wasn't so stupid or naive that he didn't realize this was the sort of thing the governor's opponent would use against him with great relish. But the least Meyers could do was cut her some slack until he knew the particulars of the situation.

"Sir," he tried again, more forcefully this time.

And again, Tom Meyers ignored him. "Do you know what this is going to do to my standing in the polls?" he demanded. Somehow, though, Miles didn't think the governor had directed the question at him so much as he had to himself. Which was good, because he immediately answered himself, too. "My opponent is going to use every opportunity he has to point out that if the governor of the great state of Texas can't even control his daughter then how can he manage the great state of Texas?"

"Sir," Miles said again, this time hurrying on when Tom Meyers opened his mouth to interrupt once more. "You've got it wrong. Totally and completely wrong. For one thing, Lanie *wasn't* undressed when those photos were taken. It's just that the camera angle makes her look as if she's undressed. Her dress was strapless, and it was short," Miles conceded. "But it was also *on*. My jacket was just longer, so the way Lanie's holding it, it hides her dress. But she was fully clothed for the entire evening, I assure you."

Miles wasn't sure if it was his imagination or not, but the governor did seem to look a bit relieved by the assurance.

So he continued. "Yes, my shirt is off in the photos," he had no choice but to acknowledge. "But that was because one of the hanging ferns had just broken free and spilled dirt down my jacket and my shirt, and I was trying to get it out of my clothes."

He braved a few steps to the governor's desk and selected one of the half-dozen newspapers lying open there.

"Look," he said, holding one up and pointing at something behind his own image in the photo. "You can see it right there. A pot hanging sideways with one of the chains that had been holding it broken away from it. I took my jacket and shirt off to get the dirt out. If you'll notice, Lanie's turned away, not looking at me. She's trying to be polite and keep the situation as *non*inflammatory as possible. She and I both were trying to show some decorum in a situation that was a little indecorous."

Tom Meyers studied the photo in silence for a moment, but Miles couldn't be sure if the man believed what he'd just told him. "It doesn't matter," the governor finally said. "It doesn't matter *what* Lanie did. It only matters how what Lanie did *looks*."

Spoken like a true politician, Miles thought. In spite of that, he told the other man, "I beg to differ, sir. In my opinion, what a person *is*, honestly and genuinely, is a hell of a lot more important than what people *think* about that person."

Meyers looked at him, seemingly tired, sad and resigned. "I agree," he said. "Unfortunately, in a situation like this, you and I are going to be in a minority. Right now," he continued, "we have to do some damage control."

"Damage control?" Miles echoed, not liking the sound of it.

"Damage control," Meyers reiterated.

He liked it even less hearing it a second time. "What are you talking about?"

"I'm talking about you and Lanie," Myers said.

"What about me and Lanie?"

For the first time since Miles's arrival, Governor Tom Meyers actually smiled. A broad, genuinely happy-looking smile. A smile that made Miles's flesh crawl. Worse than that, he walked to Miles and clapped an arm around his shoulder.

"What I'm talking about, son," Meyers said, that last word making Miles's crawling flesh turn cold, "is you doing the right thing by my daughter."

Miles hated the phrase "doing the right thing by my daughter" even more than he'd hated the phrase "damage control."

"I'm not sure I follow you, sir."

"Oh, come on, boy," Meyers said, flexing the arm on Miles's shoulder until it was almost painful. "This is Texas. We'll settle this thing the Texas way."

"The Texas way?" Miles asked, not much caring for that phrase, either.

"You know we Lone Star men always do the right thing by the women we've wronged," Meyers told him. "You and Lanie? You're going to have to get married."

Five

Miles told himself he couldn't possibly have heard correctly. For one thing, he hadn't wronged anyone. And for another, he'd decided a long time ago that he wasn't going to marry *anyone,* right *or* wronged. Yeah, what had happened with Lanie at the fund-raiser was the sort of thing that would generate gossip and innuendo, and that wasn't good for the governor at any time, especially now. But that was all that the talk would be—gossip and innuendo. The photos in the paper were suggestive, sure, but they weren't graphic or explicit. Someone with a cool head could reasonably and rationally explain what had actually happened. And Tom Meyers could do that, if he'd just keep his wits about him.

Of course, it wouldn't hurt if Miles could find Kaminski and threaten to wring the guy's scrawny little chicken neck if he didn't come clean and tell the truth about what he'd photographed that night. But that was going to have to wait, he told himself regretfully, because right now he had to focus on the gibberish the governor was spouting. The guy was off his rocker if he thought Miles and Lanie should get married over something like this.

As if reading his mind, the governor continued with a sick smile, "Oh, don't worry, son, I'm not going to stick a shotgun barrel between your shoulder blades. But I do think you should propose to the girl. At least for the sake of appearances."

"Sir, with all due respect, I really think you're overreacting about this."

"Overreacting?" the governor asked, his smile fading now. "Do you want to know what I've had to go through this morning?"

Not really, Miles thought.

"Thirty-seven phone calls from thirty-seven different newspapers," Meyers told him, anyway. "Thirty-seven," he repeated for emphasis. "Some of them as far away as Tokyo and Bangladesh. And then there are those who haven't been able to get through yet, because my line's been too busy. Hell, boy, I finally had to take the phone off the damned hook because I was about to lose my voice with all the talking."

Which meant the governor had talked to quite a few of the reporters who had called, Miles translated. Great. This was just great. The guy had already started putting his own spin on the situation, without even trying to learn the truth of what had actually happened.

"So you've already talked to the press, then," Miles said, speaking his thoughts—at least part of them—aloud.

"Hell, yes, I've already talked to the press," Meyers

said. "I didn't have much choice when they showed up right outside my door. How would it have looked if I *hadn't* talked to them?"

"It might have just looked like you were too busy to talk to them," Miles said.

Meyers shook his head vehemently. "Oh, no," he said, just as fervently. "You don't know these snakes and vipers in the media the way I do."

Wanna bet? Miles thought.

But the governor started talking again before he had a chance to get the question out. Which was just as well, all things considered.

"They would have taken silence—or worse, 'no comment'—as a confirmation that what they saw in the photographs was the truth, the whole truth and nothing but the truth. So here's the plan," the governor continued before Miles had a chance to object. "I told them you and Lanie have been secretly engaged for months, and that you're planning a small, private, Valentine's Day wedding."

"You *what?*" Miles cried.

Meyers, to his credit, didn't bat an eye. "I told them you and Lanie are engaged to be married in a few months, and that you're going to do it right here at the governor's mansion. That you were keeping it a secret because you didn't want the press to be hounding your every step. I told them you did your best to be discreet during your secret engagement, and that you were managing just fine until Saturday night. I told them that if you two were jumping the gun on the honeymoon that night, it was only because you're so crazy in love and so anxious to be married, that you just got caught up in the romance of it all."

Miles closed his eyes and muttered, "You didn't."

"I did," the governor assured him, honestly sounding proud of himself. "It'll be in all the papers tomorrow."

Miles opened his eyes and met the governor's gaze levelly. But for the life of him, he had no idea what to say.

The governor looked at his watch. "Lanie will be here in half an hour," he said. "When she gets here, I'll go over the details of your impending nuptials with you both."

"There aren't going to be any nuptials," Miles said decisively. No way was he going to go through with a cockamamy scheme like this. And Lanie wouldn't, either, he was sure.

"Of course there won't," Meyers agreed. "I told you you don't have to marry the girl. But the two of you have to get your stories straight," he went on, "if this engagement story is going to play successfully in the media spotlight. And if you value your good name, Fortune," the governor added when Miles opened his mouth to object, "you'll definitely play this engagement story successfully in the media spotlight."

Miles snapped his mouth shut again.

"Look, you'll be rewarded for your cooperation," Meyers said. "I wouldn't expect any man to surrender four months of his life for something like this without compensating him for his efforts."

"Rewarded," Miles repeated blandly. "Compensated."

"Of course," Meyers told him. "You don't think I'd make you go through all this for nothing."

"I haven't agreed to go through with anything," Miles pointed out.

The governor smiled again. "You will," he said simply. "Because once the election is over—which I *will* win, in spite of this little setback—you'll take home a nice fat check from a very appreciative man."

Now Miles's eyebrows arched to nearly his hairline. "Are you offering me a *bribe*, Governor?"

"Of course not," Meyers said. "I'm offering you payment for services rendered, the same way I'd pay my gardener for tending to my lawn."

Putting aside the crassness of the comparison, Miles said, "And just what kind of services are we talking about now?"

Meyers rocked back on his heels and stated, flat out, "If you go through with this, and pretend you're marrying my daughter, *and* convince the media that the two of you are hopelessly, legitimately in love—in a monogamous, matrimonial, all-American kind of way—then I'll give you a hundred thousand dollars."

Miles's reaction to that would have been the same if Tom Meyers had just hit him upside the head with a brick. "I beg your pardon."

"You heard me," the governor said. "There's no need for me to say it twice. Just know that if you pull this off and help me win a second term by pretending to be my daughter's fiancé, then you'll be very well compensated for having given up a few months of your life." He laughed, clearly joking when he added, "Hell, marry her for real and I'll double it."

Miles shook his head slowly, unable to believe that the governor of Texas had just offered him money—a lot of money, too, even by his standards—to pretend to be his daughter's fiancé for a couple of months. And he was surprised at just how many levels that bothered him on. Miles had never considered himself the most ethical human being on the planet. Sure, he was a moral enough guy. But his morals were pretty fluid and could be molded to fit a variety of situations. It took a lot to offend him. But he discovered he was pretty danged offended right now.

First off, the connotation of the whole thing was distasteful. Secondly, the governor was revealing himself to be a controlling little geek. Thirdly, under any other circumstances, Miles would have been delighted to accompany Lanie Meyers anywhere, at no charge whatsoever. Hell, before Kaminski had shown up that night, he'd been planning to ask her out.

Nor could Miles believe that his private life had just been aired to the press. Not that it hadn't been fodder for the media a dozen times before. He could barely attend a social event without having some mention or photograph appear in the paper the next day. But at least those accounts were true, and at least they'd been within the bounds of decency—even when the nights following those social events were anything but decent, depending on whom he'd been escorting to the event. But this…

This was too much. This had just gone too far and had gotten out of control. There was no way he was going to let anyone—not even the governor of Texas—dictate his future, real *or* imaginary. Tom Meyers was not going to make Miles Fortune out to be his future son-in-law. And not just because Miles would have too many people to explain it to, either. This didn't just affect Miles. It affected the whole Fortune clan. Because they'd all want to know why he hadn't told them about Lanie, or his upcoming wedding, or a million other things.

And there was Lanie to think about, too. She'd have as much awkwardness and explaining to do as Miles would. She'd be as uncomfortable living a lie as he would. And she probably wouldn't even be offered money by her father for doing it. Not that Miles would even consider taking money in exchange for this thing. Were he to agree to it, he meant, which he never would.

If Tom Meyers thought the press was a problem now, it was going to be even worse if they thought there was a wedding in the near future for the Government Goddess. On the other hand, if they just left it alone, what had happened Saturday night would blow over in a couple of weeks.

But, then, Tom Meyers didn't have a couple of weeks, did he? Miles reminded himself. He couldn't risk the slightest smudge of gossip or innuendo impeding his reelection. And, hey, if he was about to be the father of the bride, that gave him an appeal he didn't have otherwise. Not to mention it would deflect the media attention from the election to Lanie's wedding, something that symbolized hope and love and the American way of life.

Miles should have seen that coming from a mile away. By creating this phony engagement and upcoming wedding, Tom Meyers had just fashioned for himself something that might very well seal the election in his favor. He'd taken what could have been viewed as a licentious indiscretion of an out-of-control daughter and turned it into a sweet, impetuous, romantic interlude of a daughter in love with the man she intended to spend the rest of her life with. And in the process, he'd diverted attention from his reelection campaign and put it on Lanie's wedding instead.

Man. Tom Meyers was truly a consummate politician.

Which made Miles even more determined to not let the guy get away with it. He wasn't going to let the governor use him and Lanie to further his own agenda. No way.

When Lanie got here, between the two of them, they'd set the old man straight.

And then some.

The last thing Lanie expected to see when she entered her father's office was Miles Fortune. Oh, certainly she'd figured her father would recognize Miles from the photographs in the morning papers. Who wouldn't? The Fortunes were almost as well-known in Texas as the Meyerses were. But she'd figured her father would blame her alone for what had happened, since whenever she got into trouble, it was always her fault. She glanced down at the grubby jeans and slouchy black sweater she had thrown on, thinking this meeting would involve only her and her father, wishing now she had dressed in something a little more appropriate. Because even though Miles's clothing was no more formal than her own, he carried off his appearance with far more aplomb than she did.

Unfortunately, judging by the dark look on his face, he wasn't any happier with her at the moment than her father was. Not that any of this was her fault. She and Miles were both victims. Miles himself had stated that the photographer had been gunning for him for some time. So there was no reason for him to be glowering at her the way he was.

Nevertheless, any righteous indignation she might have been able to muster fizzled when she turned her attention to her father. She'd seen him ticked off on many occasions, most of them following some episode where she had managed to get herself into trouble. But she'd never seen him looking quite that steely before.

"Elaine Mathilda Meyers," he said in a frosty voice.

Ack. Even after her most egregious social faux pas, her

father hadn't used her full given name. He hadn't done that since she was a child.

"What the *hell* were you thinking, girl, to let something like this happen?" he asked.

Before she could even get her mouth open to respond, though, he continued, "Well, obviously you *weren't* thinking, were you? But when you let something like this happen…"

His voice trailed off, and Lanie did manage to get her mouth open to reply this time, but her father started talking again before she had the chance to say a word.

"Your friend Mr. Fortune here would have me believe that nothing happened Saturday night, that these—" he snatched up one of the many newspapers from his desk and smacked it hard "—these *photographs*—are misleading. That the two of you weren't parading around without your clothes at a public event benefiting your own father."

"That's right, Dad. We—"

"And I told Mr. Fortune," her father went on, before she could finish, "that was beside the point. Appearances matter more than deeds for political families, something I would have thought you might have learned by now."

"Actually, Dad," Lanie tried again, "I can't say I really agree with you on th—"

"It doesn't matter what you agree with me on," her father interrupted her. "All that matters is that you've put me and everyone who's worked on my campaign in a real bind. Couldn't you have at least kept your shenanigans to a minimum until after I was reelected? Couldn't you *think*, for God's sake? About someone other than *yourself* for a change?"

Lanie didn't know what to say in response to that, so she

said nothing. Her father was more upset now than usual because the election was so close. Usually, he wasn't this hot-tempered about her indiscretions. The pressure of the last few months had just built in him to a point where he was afraid he was going to lose his job, and that made him more critical than he would be under other circumstances.

"This time you've gone too far, Elaine," he continued. "You may well have cost me the election with this stunt. This is exactly the kind of thing the other party likes to see happen at this point. My opponent is going to paint you and me both in as bad a light as he can."

Lanie started to speak, thought better of it and bent her head to stare at the floor. He was right. Fair or not, her fault or not, she may have cost him the election. And there was no way she could fix that.

"So this time," her father said, his voice leveling off and quieting some, "you're going to do more than just apologize and promise to try harder next time. This time, you're going to fix things."

Lanie glanced up at that, puzzled. "What do you mean?" she asked. "How can I fix this?"

Her father looked at Miles Fortune, then back at her. Then he smiled a strange kind of smile.

"Miles has agreed to make an honest woman out of you," her father told her. "The two of you are going to get engaged. Pronto."

Miles listened closely as Governor Meyers outlined his plan once again, this time to his daughter. Nope. He didn't like it any better on second hearing. In fact, it sounded even more incredible and ridiculous. Problem now was that he had been planning on Lanie rejecting it as soundly as he had himself. But she was so quiet in the aftermath of her father's harangue, Miles feared she might never speak again.

It was bad enough that the governor had called Lanie selfish and thoughtless to Miles. But then he'd said pretty much the same things right to her face. Had she had to put up with stuff like that all her life? How had she turned out to be the sweet, articulate, fun person he'd spent the evening with two nights ago?

Miles looked at Lanie again. Gone was the laughing, outgoing, vivacious young woman he'd had such a good time with two nights ago. In her place was a timid, mousy creature not saying a word. Tom Meyers had managed to berate the spirit right out of her.

But her head snapped up at her father's decree that she and Miles were going to get engaged. He waited for her to object, waited for her to stomp her foot, waited for her to announce that there was no way she would go along with such a crazy scheme.

But she said nothing, did nothing, only dropped her gaze to the floor again without so much as acknowledging what her father had said.

Miles wished that he could read her mind. And he wished that she would speak it.

That wasn't looking likely, though. She was probably afraid to say anything. And she was probably trying to decide who would be the most formidable adversary in this situation—her father or Miles. That really wasn't a choice she should have to make.

Miles wasn't sure just when the hammer fell, when he made the decision to go along with the governor's cockamamy phony engagement to Lanie. He only knew that suddenly he was willing to do whatever it took to make

Tom Meyers leave his daughter alone. No, he wasn't responsible for what had happened Saturday night, and he wasn't responsible for the public reaction to the photos in the morning paper. But neither was Lanie. Still, when all was said and done, she was going to bear the brunt of the repercussions. Not just from her father, but from the public, too. Because however unfair it was—and it was most definitely unfair—in this society, women were the ones who paid the price for such things. Miles wasn't willing to let Lanie shoulder more than her fair share.

Hell, it would just be for a few months, right? he reassured himself. By the end of the year he and Lanie could start making noises about how all was not perfect in paradise, and they could start pulling away from each other in the public eye. Besides, how hard could it be to act as if he were in love with her and wanted to marry her? She was a beautiful, charming woman, the exact sort of woman to whom Miles was usually drawn. And he *was* drawn to her. With or without this scandal, he wouldn't have minded getting to know the governor's daughter better.

The election would be over soon. He and Lanie could bide their time for a couple of months afterward, pretending to plan a wedding, showing up at parties together, attending a few wedding-related events and businesses. They could go out on dates and do the stuff affianced people do. Then, a few weeks before the supposed wedding, one or both of them could back out, citing cold feet or a change of heart. Who'd be hurt? That kind of thing happened all the time, even with people who really did intend to get married.

Hey, it might even be kind of fun to pretend to be engaged and planning a wedding. Because wasn't that the kind of thing every confirmed bachelor spent his days fantasizing about? he thought dryly. He couldn't wait to start pondering the perfect wedding theme and going through samples of fabric swatches to pick just the right color scheme, and sampling cakes for just the most savory one—well, okay, that part might not be too bad—and registering for kitchen appliances he wanted absolutely no part of. Whoa, yeah. Just the thought of being dragged through Neiman Marcus to look at bedspreads and china patterns made his little heart go pitter-patter.

Still, he thought further, planning a wedding sure the hell wasn't the kind of thing he ever intended to do in reality, so this could be an adventure. Kind of. A safe adventure, too, since there was no danger of an outcome that left him truly married.

"It's a good idea, Lanie," he heard himself say, not sure when he'd even made the decision to speak aloud. "We should do what your father says."

Both Lanie and the governor glanced over at him, both looking very surprised by what he had said. But where Governor Meyers smiled with much contentment Lanie frowned.

"Miles, it's totally unnecessary," she said.

So she could speak to him, Miles thought, but not to her father. For some reason—a reason he figured he'd be better off not thinking too hard about—that made him happy in an odd kind of way.

"I know it's not necessary," he said. "Because nothing happened Saturday night and neither one of us owes anyone else an explanation. But this is going to cause a lot of talk, and the person who's going to end up suffering the worst consequences will be you."

And when all was said and done, maybe that was what

was at the heart of Miles's motives. It just wasn't fair that Lanie had been the one the newspaper headlines had tried hardest to hurt that morning. None had made suggestive comments about Miles's morality or his virtue, even though he'd been every bit as visible and identifiable—and *more* undressed, ironically—in the photos as she had been.

"I think we should agree to your father's proposal," he added, wincing when he heard the last word he uttered so unwittingly. "I think you should agree to my proposal," he then amended.

"What proposal?" she asked.

Miles smiled halfheartedly and crossed the room to where she stood. Dropping onto one knee, he took her hand in his and said, "Lanie Meyers, will you pretend to marry me?"

Six

Miles studied Lanie over the rim of his coffee cup and silently cursed Governor Tom Meyers. Although she'd rallied briefly after his pseudoproposal and had even managed to smile at him, now she was back to being withdrawn. Even though she'd reluctantly agreed to her father's plan, she seemed none too enthusiastic about carrying it out.

He still couldn't believe Meyers had offered to pay him six figures. Like hell. No way was he taking a dime from that man. Miles was doing this for Lanie, and Lanie alone.

So now here they were, sitting in a coffee shop near the state capitol building, where Miles had suggested they go to regroup after they'd left the governor's office.

"You really don't have to do this," Lanie said softly, staring down into her coffee mug.

Which, Miles noted, she had yet to touch. He had ordered from the barista while she found a table—in the very back of the shop, he'd noticed—and he'd brought both mugs to the table. She was sitting now as she had been ever since, with her head bent and her hands in her lap.

"You don't have to do it, either," he pointed out.

Still not looking up, she said, "Actually, I do. I owe my father at least that much."

"You don't owe your father anything," Miles replied.

"He's really not as bad as you think he is," she said softly.

"I don't know," Miles countered. "He wasn't exactly Mr. Nice Guy in there."

"It's just because of the election," she told him. "It hasn't been easy on him the last few months, with his opponent gaining on him the way he has been. Don't get me wrong," she added, holding up a hand when Miles started to object. "He's definitely overreacting to this. But under normal circumstances, he'd be much more reasonable, and much less…" She paused, evidently not knowing exactly what word she was looking for.

But that was okay, because Miles supplied it readily enough. "Obnoxious?"

Lanie smiled at that, and he felt a little better. "Yeah, okay, he was that. But really, Miles, if you could see him under normal circumstances, you'd see that he's not a bad guy. This tiny margin in the polls just has him crazy right now, and he's not been himself."

"That doesn't give him an excuse to try and manipulate us."

"No, it doesn't, but thank you for going along with his scheme, however crazy it is. I appreciate it. Especially since you're under no obligation. To me *or* my father."

"Well, not your father, no," Miles agreed. "But I do feel obligated to you."

"Well, you shouldn't," she insisted.

"Hey, what happened Saturday night was nothing you courted, nothing you caused and nothing you deserved. Nothing happened that night, Lanie. Your father should realize that, and he should explain it to the media. He shouldn't ask you to lie to cover up a nonevent."

Not that politicians asking others to lie for them was anything new, Miles thought. But it was one thing to ask one's professional associates to do it and another thing entirely to insist one's own daughter do it. Especially when there was no reason for the lie to begin with.

"Well, thank you anyway," she said. "I'm sure my father appreciates it."

"I'm not doing it for your father," Miles told her.

"Right. Of course," she said. "I wasn't thinking. When all is said and done, you have as much to lose here as my father does. It's your reputation on the line as much as his."

"Hey, my reputation sucks," Miles said frankly. "I'm not doing this for me, either."

This time, when Lanie looked up at him, she met his gaze full-on, and she didn't look away. She even roused a small smile for him, one that made Miles's heart do a funny little flip-flop unlike anything he'd felt before. She did have a very sweet smile, he thought. And she was very pretty. Even now, early in the morning, with no makeup and her hair pulled back into a less-than-tidy ponytail, wearing faded jeans and a shapeless black sweater. Usually Miles didn't even notice women like that. This morning, though, with Lanie, for some reason he'd barely noticed anything else.

"It won't be that bad," he told her, surprised to discover he spoke the truth. "It's not like we're really engaged. Like your dad said, all we have to do is make a good show of it, and after the first of the year, after your dad is sworn in and all that, we can split amicably and tell everyone it was just one of those things."

He leaned back in his chair and sipped his coffee. "The hardest part will be the press conference your father is organizing for tomorrow morning," he added, recalling that last announcement of her father's. "You and I have less than twenty-four hours to figure out how we're going to make this look convincing, and we barely know each other."

Lanie reached for her coffee, finally, but all she did was run the pad of her finger around the rim of her mug. Miles found the gesture inordinately interesting, and watched, fascinated, as she completed it. As he observed her finger making a slow circle around the edge of her cup, all he could do was wonder how it would feel to have her drawing another such circle on him. Preferably while he was naked.

That was when he started to think that maybe this wasn't going to be as easy as he'd first thought.

"I'd think the hardest part would be how this is going to cut big-time into your social life," she said. "I mean, you're not going to be able to date anyone for months."

Miles smiled reassuringly, nudging thoughts of nakedness and Lanie's fingers to the back of his mind. Well, kind of. It was always hard to completely banish naked thoughts once they occurred. "Sure I can date," he told Lanie. "I'll be dating you."

She actually blushed at that, then glanced away again, but this time it was with a smile, and this time she looked back right away. "But what will your girlfriend say?"

"I don't have a girlfriend," he told her.

Which was also true. In fact, the closest thing Miles had had to a girlfriend recently had been out of his life for almost a year. And, truth be told, he hadn't been that sorry to see her go. Since then, he'd dated freely and without inhibition, but never one woman for very long. He'd attended the governor's bash stag, after all.

That didn't mean, however, that Lanie didn't have a boyfriend, he realized then. And he was surprised at how much the possibility of such a thing bothered him. "What about you?" he asked.

She looked confused. "What about me?"

"What will you tell your boyfriend?"

She shrugged one shoulder and let it drop, then lifted her coffee cup. "I don't have a boyfriend," she said without concern.

Miles felt himself relax…and then wondered why he had tensed up in the first place. "So that works out well," he said.

She nodded as she completed a sip of her coffee. "Except that we're going to have to come up with some reasonable explanation for why no one has seen us together before now. I mean, we've evidently fallen in love if we're planning to get married. How are we supposed to explain that, when we haven't even said a word to our families or friends about each other?"

Good question, Miles thought. He wished he had a good answer to go with it. Especially with that press conference looming at which he and Lanie were supposed to officially announce their engagement, now that they'd been outed.

"Well, I guess we have a whole day to figure that out, don't we?" he told her. "Good thing neither one of us has to work today."

Which was kind of a dumb thing to say, Miles realized right away. He *was* supposed to be working today, because he was supposed to be leaving Austin this afternoon and returning to Red Rock. And he honestly didn't think Lanie had a job. The fact that he would utter something dumb in the presence of a pretty woman should probably have tipped him off to something significant. But for the life of him, he didn't know what. He was too busy looking at Lanie and marveling again at how good she looked under such lousy circumstances, and how she probably looked even better when she was naked and— He stopped, sure that could lead nowhere good.

He traveled back to his original train of thought. Asking her to spend the day with him, which seemed like a very good idea. And tomorrow, too, he thought, since they had the press conference in the morning, and there was no reason why they should part ways after that. Of course, now he'd have to reschedule his flight home until later in the week, Miles realized. Or better still, he could drive the short distance back to Red Rock. Maybe he could even take Lanie home with him. He needed to introduce her to his family, after all. The Fortunes would kill him if he came home engaged and didn't bring his fiancée with him.

"You're not busy today, are you?" he asked belatedly, still a little preoccupied with what he'd need to be doing in the days ahead and, to be truthful, with thoughts of what Lanie would look like naked....

To his irritation, she nodded in response to his question. "As a matter of fact, I am busy," she told him.

Well, hell, he thought. Then he'd just have to find the guy she was going to be busy with and scare him off.

But she smiled in a way then that chased every menacing thought out of Miles's head…and chased all the air out of his lungs in a swift, debilitating *whoosh.*

"I'll be spending the day," she told him, "with my fiancé."

Oh. Well, then, that was all right. Miles smiled, too.

"But do you mind if I change first?" she said, glancing down at her attire. "I'm not exactly fit to be seen in public right now."

Which really wasn't a problem, Miles thought, since he wouldn't have minded a little private time with Lanie instead. He wasn't exactly dressed for a day out, either.

"We don't have to go out," he told her, speaking his thoughts aloud. "In fact, it might be better if we kept a low profile until tomorrow."

He could tell by her expression that she saw the sense in what he was saying. He could also tell by her expression that she didn't look forward to private time in quite the way Miles did. In fact, she looked downright spooked by the idea of such a thing.

Telling himself he shouldn't be offended, since she really didn't know him all that well yet, Miles offered, "Look, why don't we just head out of Austin for the day and find some quiet park or some out-of-the-way place where we can take a walk and have some lunch and do some talking and figure out the basics so we can make it through the press conference tomorrow. You look fine for that."

Hell, she looked fine period, Miles thought. But considering that deer-in-the-headlights look she had on her face, he should probably keep the observation to himself for now.

"And then tomorrow," he continued, "after the press conference, you can come with me to Red Rock and spend a few days at the ranch. The Flying Aces Ranch," he clarified, "the one I own with my brother Clyde. Clyde and his wife, Jessica, will be there," he hastened to add so that Lanie wouldn't be concerned that the two of them would be alone. "The rest of the family can come over one day while you're there. They're going to want to meet you. At the Flying Aces, we'll have privacy and the press will have to leave us alone. We can spend a few days there figuring out just how the hell we're going to keep this thing credible for the next few months."

Where he had thought she would be relieved by the invitation, instead she only grew more agitated.

"What?" he asked. "What's wrong?"

"I just remembered something," she told him.

"What?"

She nibbled her lip nervously, in a way that made an urgent heat go splashing through Miles's belly, even though there was nothing even remotely sexual in the gesture. "I've sort of, um, already met your sister?" she said, posing the statement as a question due to what was obviously anxiety.

The news came as a surprise to Miles, but he didn't see why it would be a problem. "So?" he asked.

"So it was just earlier this month," Lanie said.

Okay, so that might be a problem, but he couldn't see it as being an insurmountable one. "That's okay," he said. "We would have still been keeping our relationship a secret at that point."

"But I sorta had brunch with her that day," Lanie said. "And with Ryan and Lily, too, at the Double Crown."

Oh, Miles thought. That might be a bit of a problem. Violet would kill him when she found out she'd had brunch with his fiancée and no one had bothered to mention the engagement.

"I'll deal with it," he said. And somehow, he would. "I'll call home tonight to prepare everybody for what's going to come out at the press conference. By the time we get to the ranch, their ruffled feathers ought to be smoothed over."

Right, Miles thought. Like he believed that. Still, there was no reason to make Lanie more worried than she already clearly was. He could handle Violet. Probably. Maybe. If he caught her in a weak moment…

"Thanks," Lanie told him. "I'm really sorry this is going to cause you so much trouble."

Miles waved off her concern literally. It was odd how easy he was taking this all, given that he normally didn't like it when his life got turned upside down.

Later, he told himself, he'd think about why. As soon as he stopped thinking about how pretty Lanie Meyers was.

"You'll love the Flying Aces," he said, proud of the ranch and anxious to show it off. Especially to Lanie.

"I can't wait to see it. And I look forward to seeing Violet again. She and I had a nice chat. And not just about Ryan's party next month."

Right, Miles thought. Now he remembered. Ryan Fortune, his distant cousin, was being honored by the governor because of all the volunteer work he did on behalf of the environment. All his life Ryan had been a notorious do-gooder, working on everything from stocking food banks to hosting the San Antonio Boys and Girls Clubs for a summer camp at the ranch, to donating regularly—and substantially—to Mothers Against Drunk Driving. That last was a result of Ryan's having lost his brother ten years ago to a car accident that had involved drunk driving.

The party would be at Miles's brother Steven's ranch, and was promising to be a major event. The guest list included everybody who was anybody in the state of Texas. Politicians, oilmen, cattlemen, captains of industry, giants of technology, movie stars, television stars, you name it. And, of course, every Fortune they could find. Miles was glad all the preparation had been left to someone else, and that the only thing he'd be obligated to do was show up for a good time. Of course, now he'd be attending the party with his fiancée. And for some reason, that made an already spectacular-sounding evening suddenly seem even more dazzling.

"And I look forward to showing you the ranch," he said, getting the conversation back on track. "Just leave everything at the Flying Aces to me once we arrive, all right?"

Lanie nodded. "Thanks. I've heard a lot about the Flying Aces. It will be nice to finally see it."

"Yeah, well, it's nothing compared to Ryan's place," Miles said. "But we like it."

We being Miles and the other Fortunes who would be on hand when he and Lanie arrived tomorrow. Which meant they really did have to come up with at least some small part of their history as a couple before they went to the Flying Aces. Well, for that reason, and for the press conference, too.

He drained the last of his coffee and watched as Lanie did likewise. "Shall we?" he asked then, sweeping his hand toward the coffee shop exit.

Lanie nodded and smiled. "I surrender myself to your capable hands," she said.

Even though there was absolutely nothing in the comment that might be misconstrued as sexual in nature, Miles suddenly received a very vivid—very graphic—mental image of just what it might be like to have Lanie Meyers surrendering to his capable hands. And what it might be like for him to surrender to hers. And then what it might be like for both of them to spend the rest of the night letting each others' hands do whatever the hell they pleased.

He squeezed his eyes shut tight in an effort to banish his wayward thoughts again. Unfortunately—or maybe fortunately, depending on your point of view—that only made the scenes more vivid and graphic.

And all he could think then was that it was a shame he was a phony fiancé. Because suddenly he was in the mood for a very real honeymoon.

In spite of the cool air and the fat gray clouds overhead, it was a lovely day for a walk in the park. Or maybe it was just being in the park with Miles that made it such a lovely day, Lanie couldn't help thinking as she strode alongside him in comfortable silence. He was just so handsome, and he'd been so sweet to her all day. Especially in light of the circumstances. Any other guy would have been furious to have his life overrun the way her father had overrun Miles's. But he seemed to be taking it all in stride, didn't seem to be bothered in the slightest that he was going to have to put his life on hold for months because of something for which he had been in no way responsible.

He just seemed like such a decent guy, she thought. And the fact that that decent guy came wrapped in such an incredible package just made Lanie marvel more at her good luck.

Good luck, she repeated to herself, smiling inwardly at the thought. Good fortune. All things considered, she hadn't been too lucky lately. Her seemingly naked body had been splashed across virtually every newspaper and television channel in the country over the last twenty-four hours, she may well have ended her father's political career, she was an embarrassment to her family and the entire state of Texas… Yet here she was thinking she was lucky.

She glanced up at Miles again, from beneath her lashes, at the espresso eyes and bittersweet-chocolate hair, at the chiseled jaw and the ruddy complexion, at the broad shoulders and solid chest and arms…

She bit back a sigh. Yes, indeed. She was an extraordinarily lucky woman.

She couldn't remember the last time she'd indulged in such a simple pleasure as taking a walk. When had her life become so full that she'd stopped having time for such things? she wondered. Giving the question some thought, she began to realize she'd never had time for such pursuits, not really. For as long as she could remember, her life had been rigidly scheduled. As much as she'd insisted she wanted to strike out on her own as an adult, she realized now that there was very little in her life that was her own. Too often, she still put her parents' requirements—and her father's career—ahead of herself.

"Penny for your thoughts," Miles said suddenly, pulling her out of her musing.

She smiled up at him. "Just a penny?" she asked. "Boy, I really must not be a very interesting person."

He smiled back. "On the contrary, Ms. Meyers, I think you're fascinating."

"Then I'd think my thoughts would be worth at least a couple of bucks," she said.

"Okay," he conceded readily. "A couple of bucks for your thoughts."

She shrugged. "I wasn't really thinking about anything much," she hedged.

"Oh, and for that I paid a couple of bucks? That's not even worth a penny."

She laughed. "All right. I was just thinking that you seem to be taking all this remarkably well," she told him, backing up to what she'd been thinking originally and neglecting to mention everything else. "Most men would never have agreed to go along with my father's ridiculous idea."

He shrugged, but instead of commenting on her statement, said, "If we're going to make it through that press conference tomorrow morning, we should probably get at least a few details of our relationship hammered out today."

Lanie nodded and tucked her hands into the pockets of her blue jeans. "So how did we meet?" she asked. "If you live near San Antonio, and I've been in Austin the last four years, how could our paths have crossed before Saturday night?"

"A party," Miles said automatically. "You and I both have a reputation for socializing. That makes the most sense."

"But then there would be witnesses to our meeting," she said. "What if the press tries to find some and no one steps forward? Will that make them suspicious?"

"Okay. Then how about we met through a mutual acquaintance?" Miles asked. "You know anyone we could pull into this farce who would go along with it? Pretend to play matchmaker?"

Lanie gave that some thought before shaking her head. "Not really. I have a lot of friends, but I'm not sure I'd trust any of them with something like this."

He eyed her curiously. "You don't have any close, intimate friends?" he asked.

"None that close," she told him, wondering why he found that so interesting. "Why?"

He shrugged again, but the gesture this time seemed less casual somehow. "No reason."

"Do you know anyone who could help us?" she asked, still eyeing him suspiciously.

"I suppose I could get one of my brothers to do it," he said.

Her eyes widened in panic.

"Don't worry," he hastened to reassure her. "Both Clyde and Steven are totally trustworthy. The three of us have covered for each other in more ways than you can imagine, and none of us has ever ratted out the others."

His smile turned absolutely sublime at that, and Lanie found herself smiling back. "What are you remembering?" she asked. "What kind of nefarious little things did you and your identical brothers get into when you were kids?"

He laughed lightly, a soft, affectionate laugh just brimming with obvious love for the two men who were his mirror images. "Well," he said, "being a triplet definitely had its advantages while we were growing up. Clyde and Steven and I used to trade off identities fairly regularly, whenever one of us needed an out of some kind."

"Like when?" Lanie asked, liking this side of him.

"Well, let's see," he said. "I remember in second grade, I once took a spelling test for Clyde because he was having trouble with the word *organization*. And then Clyde returned the favor in fourth grade, taking a math test for me, because I was having trouble with long division."

Lanie laughed at that. "You bad boys," she said. "Just promise me you never took each other's places with girls."

"Well, as a matter of fact…" he said, blushing.

"You didn't!" Lanie gasped, scandalized, but unable to hide her laughter.

"Well, it wasn't often," Miles said in his defense. "But once, when we were sixteen, I took out a girl and pretended to be Steven when he found himself double-booked without realizing it. And Steven took turns as both me and Clyde on more than one occasion."

"I can't believe you guys," Lanie said, still smiling.

"Just childish pranks," Miles said. "But I agree they were in no way ethical. But try telling that to a bunch of kids."

Lanie thought about her own childhood, and about how she *had* been ethical growing up. She'd had to be. Her father never would have allowed her to step out of line. She'd had it impressed on her from the day she was old enough to walk and talk that she had to be the very picture of decency, morality, courtesy and good behavior, no matter what. There had been no childish pranks in her childhood, harmless or otherwise. Her parents wouldn't have tolerated it. Which was maybe another reason why she found herself in…situations as an adult.

She envied Miles then, wishing she'd had the kind of upbringing he had, with lots of siblings and mischief. She couldn't imagine what that must have been like.

"The point is," he continued, pulling Lanie back to the matter at hand, "even now the three of us keep our lips buttoned, not just about what went on in the past, but what goes on in the present. I trust both of my brothers totally and without hesitation, the same way they trust me. None of us would ever betray the others, even if our lives depended on it. We're just that tightly bound."

"That must be nice," Lanie said.

Miles nodded decisively. "It is."

"So, then, which one of them will you ask to be our backup?"

He gave that some thought for a moment. "Well, Steven's been in Austin since he started building the ranch," he finally said. "He could have met you while he was at some function or another. We can figure it out when I talk to him. And then, when you were in San Antonio for something, he and I could have been together and bumped into you somewhere there. And that could be when he introduced us, and we were immediately attracted to each other and started dating. But we did it on the sly because we'd both been burned by the press before, and we were afraid of it happening again. We didn't even tell Steven about it, so he wouldn't have to lie for us more than that once. But he'll be able to vouch for us having met last summer."

Lanie had started nodding as Miles spoke. "That would work," she said. "I spent a long weekend with my mother in San Antonio at the end of June for a fund-raiser. We could have met then."

"Of course, there's still the small matter of us living in two different, and not especially close, cities," he pointed out.

"Yeah, but we can gloss over that," she said. "I've been doing a lot of traveling with my parents this year, stumping for dad's reelection. Maybe you met me on the campaign trail when you could."

He nodded. "I've done a fair bit of traveling over the last six months, too," he said. "Looking at potential breeding stock. So we could just say that we both arranged our schedules to coincide with each other's travels, and got together whenever we could."

Lanie was warming to the story now. "I think that would work well. But that's going to mean that we've only been dating for a few months," she said. "And sporadically at that. My father told the reporters that we've been engaged for more than a month. So we must have decided to get married after only dating for two or three months. Will that wash? I mean, could we really have fallen in love that quickly? The kind of love that makes two people want to spend the rest of their lives together?"

Miles lifted one shoulder and let it drop. "Sure, why not?"

He was amazed to hear himself capitulate so easily to such a suggestion. He'd never thought that kind of love even existed, let alone happened so quickly. He'd always thought people who wanted to get married and spend the rest of their lives together were just kidding themselves. That it was just wishful thinking at best, self-delusion at worst. No one, he'd been convinced—*no one*—was truly able to give that much of himself to another human being. People didn't get married because they were in love, he'd always thought. They got married because they were lonely. Or bored. Or desperate. Or succumbing to social mores that had gone out of fashion sometime during the last century.

Suddenly, though, for some reason, he was totally able to believe that people fell in love virtually overnight, the kind of love that transcended all time, the kind of love that led to the most nauseatingly clichéd happily-ever-after.

He groaned inwardly. No way was he going to survive this phony engagement with his manhood intact.

But here was the kicker: In a way, he kind of didn't care.

"I'll have to talk to Steven first," he said, "tell him what's up before the press conference tomorrow, so he can back us up after we tell our story. He can be as surprised as everyone else by the announcement of our engagement," he added. "But I figure he has the right to know in advance that he's the one responsible for getting us together. I'll call him tonight and go over the details with him. Now you and I just need to hammer out the details."

By the end of the day, they had the biggest ones worked out. And they were delighted to discover that there had, in fact, been several occasions over the past few months when the two of them were in the same city at the same time—or close enough to each other, geographically speaking, that meeting in some clandestine place wouldn't have been impossible.

"It's almost," Lanie said with a smile when they realized it, "as if we were destined to meet at some point and kept missing each other until it finally happened Saturday night."

Destined, Miles repeated to himself, a shiver of something both wholly scary and strangely enjoyable winding its way down his spine. Now, there was an interesting concept.

What it all boiled down to was that, however unlikely it might be, if any overly enthusiastic member of the press corps became suspicious about the circumstances of the relationship, a check into the travels of Lanie and Miles would provide the investigator with enough evidence to conclude that it was entirely possible for the two of them to have been meeting while on the road. And hey, at this point, they would take whatever they could get in the corroboration department.

It was growing dark by the time they finally started winding down. For some reason, though, Miles was in no hurry to get back to Austin. Or even Red Rock, for that matter. It had just been too nice a day with only the two of them. The same way it had been Saturday night. He'd been wondering if maybe that night had just been an aberration, if maybe he'd just had one too many bourbons in him, and that was what had buffed the edges off of the evening and made it seem nicer than most. Now, though, he realized it was Lanie who'd buffed off those edges. Lanie who had made the time pass so much more pleasantly than usual. Lanie who had made the occasion enjoyable.

And as they ambled back to where they'd left his car in a secluded spot near the park's entrance, Miles thought of one more thing that they needed to get straight before tomorrow morning. So he slowed his pace and silently willed her to do the same, until he'd brought both of them to a stop near a copse of aspens. A cool autumn breeze swept through the trees as they halted, sending a shiver of golden, feather-shaped leaves cascading around them. In the amber light of the fast-descending dusk, Miles took both of Lanie's hands in his and said, "There's something else we need to be prepared for tomorrow."

She glanced down at their hands, then back up at his face, eyeing him curiously. "What?"

He wasn't sure what was the best way to broach the subject, so he just said outright, "People are going to expect us to..." He sighed as he tried to figure out the best way to phrase it. "To be...physically demonstrative," he finally got out.

He'd feared Lanie would panic at the realization that the two of them would, at some point, have to engage in some kind of public display of affection, however innocent and however brief. But he knew it was a legitimate concern. People would be watching them now. If they were so in love that they couldn't wait to get married, then they sure wouldn't be able to keep their hands off of each other. Especially since that was what Lanie's father had stressed to the press in the first place.

"I'm sorry," he added immediately, "I know it's kind of awkward. But that has to have occurred to you, too, by now. That everyone's going to be expecting us to act like an engaged couple. As it is, according to the press, we're already acting like a honeymooning couple."

"It did occur to me," Lanie admitted. But she looked relieved instead of fearful, and Miles felt his tension ease up some. "But I didn't know if it was something that you'd given any thought to. And I wasn't sure how to bring it up."

Not given thought to getting physical with Lanie Meyers? Hell, he'd been wondering what it would be like to touch her since the two of them had shared that silent toast at her father's fund-raiser Saturday night. But he sure as hell hadn't figured it would come to this—that people were assuming he'd already been physical with her lots of times. Especially since, until this moment, the two of them had barely touched hands.

"So what do you think we should do about it?" he asked.

Her expression was philosophical. Not exactly the way a man hoped a woman would feel about getting physical with him.

"I guess the sooner we start practicing, the better," she said. She turned her wrist and looked at her watch. "The press conference is in a little over sixteen hours," she told him. "We probably shouldn't wait till the last minute."

He couldn't believe she was being so matter-of-fact about it. She talked as if kissing him were something she needed to pencil in on her busy agenda and get over with as soon as possible so she'd have one less thing to do today. Then again, he asked himself, how else was she supposed to act? He hadn't exactly introduced the topic in a way that wasn't businesslike.

Fine, then, he thought. If she wanted to just go ahead and get it over with, he'd go ahead and get it over with. So, without further hesitation, he pulled her into his arms and kissed her.

He had intended for it to be a soft, gentle, tentative kiss, one meant to give them both an opportunity to get used to the feel of each other. And really, it did start off that way. But it only took a moment for Miles to realize that kissing Lanie was different from kissing other women. He wasn't sure how, or why, or what it was that made her feel that way. He only knew that it was true. Lanie was different. And because of that, the way he responded to her was different, too. Instead of controlling the kiss, as he was usually able to do with women, Miles lost himself to it.

Vaguely, he felt himself release her hands from his so that he could curl his fingers around her warm nape and pull her head closer to his. He brushed his lips over hers lightly, once, twice, three times, four, loving the feel of her warm, soft sigh against his mouth. He felt her hands curl over his shoulders and drew her closer still, roping his arm around her waist, tangling his fingers in the hair just above her nape. Lanie, too, draped her arms around his neck, then tilted her head under his. Miles took advantage of her new position to deepen the kiss, slipping his tongue into her mouth to taste her more fully. She surged her body forward when he did, tangling her tongue with his, kissing him back with equal passion.

And then the two of them were standing there in the golden twilight, the ocher and sienna and scarlet leaves raining down around them, hands tangling in each other's hair, fingers bunching the fabric of each other's clothes, mouths locked in heated exploration, bodies on fire with need. That was when Miles forgot all about where they were, because suddenly he couldn't think, couldn't form a single, coherent idea in his brain. All he could do was feel—the way his blood raced through his veins like a hot, raging river, the way his heart pounded in his chest like a jackhammer, the way heat pooled deep in his belly, demanding a response. How soft Lanie's skin was beneath his fingers, how silky was the hair falling over the back of his hand, how erotic was the thrust of her breasts against his chest and the press of her thighs against his. And God help him, he never wanted those feelings to stop. Somehow, he wanted to hold Lanie Meyers like this forever.

But just as the realization exploded in his brain, Lanie was pulling away from him, jerking herself backward and gasping for breath. Reluctantly—miraculously—Miles allowed her to retreat without following. She took three giant steps backward, curling one arm over her midsection, pressing the back of the other hand to her mouth. Her eyes were wide and dark, though whether that was a result of passion or fear, he honestly couldn't have said. For long moments they only stared at each other in silence, their breathing ragged and labored. Miles fancied he could feel the air fairly crackling between them with whatever it was that had been generated inside them. He supposed that, whatever it was, it had to go somewhere, since both of them obviously needed to let it go.

"Okay," Lanie finally said, the word coming out a bit hoarse. "That was, um… That was pretty good. That was pretty convincing."

Yeah, I'll say, Miles thought. Aloud, though, he only replied, "Yeah, I think we've got the physical displays of affection part of our show down pretty well."

She smiled at that, a weak, timid kind of smile, but a smile nonetheless. She said nothing, however, and Miles found that he really wished he could tell what she was thinking.

He glanced up at the darkening sky overhead. "It's getting late," he said. "We should probably be getting back."

She nodded at that and, after only a small hesitation, strode forward to join him again. But she kept her distance, he noted. Earlier, as they'd walked together, her body had constantly brushed against his, and his against hers. He'd liked it, though, had liked how comfortable and natural it felt, touching her so innocently. Now, however, she maintained a good six inches of space between their bodies. Probably, he couldn't help thinking, because of the way they had just responded to each other. At this point, any touching they might do would feel anything but innocent.

Great, he thought as he opened the car door for Lanie and watched her fold herself inside. He was engaged to be married to a woman who totally turned him on. And none of it—none of it—was real.

It was going to be an interesting engagement.

Seven

The morning of the press conference dawned gray and chilly and rainy, almost as if it were a manifestation of Lanie's mood. The warmth she had felt the night before in Miles's arms had vanished, to be replaced by a chilly fear generated by having to stand in front of so many people with her father and Miles, and telling a big, fat, whopping lie. And it wasn't just because she didn't like lying—especially to the public at large—but because, after last night, she honestly wasn't sure what was true and what was false anymore.

She was still reeling from Miles's kiss. Although she hadn't slept much last night, what dreams she'd dreamed had been full of him. She could still feel the press of his solid arms encircling her, could still smell the cold leather smell of him and taste the hot coffee taste of him. She remembered the sound of his breathing mingling with hers, and how it escalated along with her own the longer the embrace went on. She remembered, too, how both of them had started to lose control, how her fingers had tangled in his hair and his hand had crept over her rib cage to settle beneath the curve of her breast. And she remembered how awkwardly they had sprung apart when they realized what they were doing, the way two affianced people would never, ever do.

She hoped they could pull this thing off today. Already, though, she felt restless and uncomfortable, and Miles wasn't even here yet. She wasn't sure she'd even be able to look him in the eye this morning after what had happened last night. How were they supposed to convince the press that they were in love and engaged if they couldn't even make eye contact?

Her gaze trailed to her bedroom window, glazed now with the morning rain. Maybe the weather would hinder visibility and make this photo opportunity less opportune. At least she and Miles would have an excuse for looking dispirited. It was literally raining on their parade. Too, the change of weather gave her an excuse to wear gloves. She'd realized last night as she was lying in bed trying not to think about Miles and worrying about what the morning would bring that she had yet something else to concern her, in addition to the host of other problems lurking just around the corner.

She didn't have an engagement ring.

The engagement ring was almost as important as the bridal gown when it came to society weddings. Any society columnist worth his or her salt would ask to see and photograph the ring. And Lanie couldn't think of a single reason—well, a plausible reason, at any rate—why she didn't have one. Yes, she could excuse having not worn one before today as a part of the whole keep-the-wedding-a-secret-from-the-press thing. But now that she and Miles were out of the closet on that score, there would be no reason for her not to wear her ring. Especially to the press conference whose sole purpose was to announce her engagement. And since she was the governor's daughter and Miles was a Texas Fortune, the ring in question would have to be nothing short of spectacular.

Not that it absolutely had to be a diamond—though certainly that would be preferable in a traditional state like Texas. But even barring that, none of the rings she owned was in any way special enough that one might pass as an engagement ring.

She glanced at her watch as she put the finishing touches on her makeup before donning the pink-and-black-checked suit with fringed skirt she'd opted to wear for the press conference. One hour, she thought. She had one hour to come up with a good reason for why her fiancé hadn't given her a ring. Because as sweet as Miles was, this just wasn't the sort of thing that would occur to him.

One hour, she repeated to herself. It was going to be a long morning.

"As you all know," the governor began, smiling the sort of smile politicians did when they slipped into their own private reality, the one that had nothing to do with real reality, "when I ran for the office of governor the first time, I vowed that I would be as honest as the day is long."

That was a phrase Miles never had been able to figure out. Did that mean he promised to be honest for only twenty-four hours out of his entire term? Or did it mean he would be honest for one single day, but no one would ever know which day it was? Would he only lie after dark? It was actually a pretty good phrase for politicians to use, he couldn't help thinking, since, when all was said and done, it made no sense whatsoever.

"Well, now I have to confess to being a little dishonest about something," Tom said, still smiling. He held up one hand with thumb and index finger nearly touching. "This much dishonest," he added with a chuckle. The crowd of reporters and photographers in the audience chuckled obediently in response. "But there was a good reason for my secrecy, and the secret had nothing to do with the great state of Texas or the great people of Texas."

Here, he paused and turned to Lanie and Miles, extending a hand toward them in a way that said, "Come on over here, you young people." So, with one brief glance at each other—almost as if it were choreographed along with the rest of the governor's speech, Miles couldn't help thinking—he and Lanie covered the few steps necessary to bring them next to Tom Meyers.

"You all know my daughter, Lanie," Tom said, speaking to the media representatives again. "And I think most of you also know Miles Fortune," he added. "What you may not have known until this morning, or should I say until *yesterday* morning—" his wink and grin sent the expected ripple of laughter over the crowd "—is that Lanie and Miles also know each other and have for several months now."

He smiled warmly at Lanie and Miles again, and Miles couldn't help but be impressed by the man's showmanship. You never would have guessed that barely twenty-four hours ago, the guy had been nearly apoplectic and throwing around threats and blackmail offers.

"And I don't think it would be exaggerating," Tom said to the crowd, "to say they made quite an impression on each other from the very first meeting. Right, kids?" He suddenly turned to look at Miles and Lanie again.

"Right, Dad," Lanie replied automatically, smiling what looked like a genuinely delighted smile.

"You know it, Mr. Meyers," Miles threw in for good measure.

"Such an impression," the governor went on, scarcely acknowledging either one of them, "that they fell head over heels in love and knew pretty quickly that they wanted to make it permanent."

At this, several photographers lifted their cameras to snap stills. Lanie lifted a hand to wave, as if the reaction were automatic, so Miles did, too. Snap. Snap. Snap. Flash. Flash. Flash.

"But see, this is why they kept it a secret," the governor said in response to the photographers, shaking a playful finger at them as he smiled more broadly. "Because they knew you people would want to document their every move. And, understandably, they wanted to let this thing unfold in private. So when they came to me and Luanne earlier this month and said they were planning a Valentine's Day wedding, they swore us to secrecy, too. Not just because they wanted to be left alone, but because they understood the demands of my campaign and the importance of the upcoming election."

Oh, bravo, Miles silently applauded the governor. *Way to bring it back to yourself, big guy.*

At that point, the governor went on about his campaign for few minutes—hey, never miss an opportunity to do a little self-promotion, Miles thought wryly—then finally returned to the reason for the press conference. He spoke briefly and vaguely about Miles and Lanie's whirlwind romance, about the Valentine's Day wedding they hoped to have at the governor's mansion, and about how proud he was of his daughter and her fella. Yeah, he actually used the word *fella,* and it was all Miles could do not to flinch at hearing himself referred to in such a way.

Finally, the governor began to wind down, and Miles began to breathe a sigh of relief that it was almost over. No sooner had the governor concluded his speech, however, than the questions began, one after the other, with the rapidity of a submachine gun.

"When's the wedding date?" asked one reporter.

Already answered, Miles thought. There was always someone who wasn't paying attention.

"Will you be wearing full-length or tea-length?" asked another.

Not that Miles had a clue what the hell the woman was talking about.

"How many attendants will you have?" asked a woman in back.

Jeez, Miles thought. The governor had just said it was going to be a small wedding with only immediate family and a few friends. Do the math. Even he knew better than to ask a question like that.

"Where will the wedding take place if your father loses the election, Lanie?"

Oh, well, that wasn't in very good taste, was it?

"Where's the ring, Lanie?"

"Yeah, we want to see the ring!" shouted another who was waving a camera.

Ah. Now that was a question worth asking, Miles

thought. When he looked over at Lanie, though, he saw her go pale.

"I have it right here," Miles piped up before Lanie could say a word.

He'd been anticipating the question, even if she hadn't, ever since he'd woken up in the middle of the night with a start at the realization that women expected jewelry for events like engagements. Hell, women expected jewelry for events like breathing. Even more to the point, reporters expected to see jewelry.

And, man, he hoped Lanie appreciated the trouble he'd gone to to find an engagement ring in time for the press conference today. It wasn't like he could just pop into a local jeweler's on the way. That would have made the news as surely as the compromising photos of him and Lanie had. He could just see the headline now: Fortune Fiancé Fails to Find Fob For Frau! Nope, couldn't have that. So he'd gotten up well before daybreak and had driven fifty miles one way to see a friend of his in New Braunfels who owned a jeweler's, had roused the guy from his bed, sworn him to secrecy and driven them both to the shop, where Miles had hastily chosen something that would represent his phony, undying love and commitment to a woman he didn't know well at all.

Not an easy task.

He'd barely made it back to Austin in time for the press conference. Still, he thought he'd done well, opting for a one-carat, square-cut diamond nestled in a filigreed platinum setting. Even knowing Lanie for as short a time as he had, he didn't see her as the ostentatious sort. Quality over quantity, that kind of thing. And the ring really was exquisite. Both contemporary and traditional, sophisticated and innocent. It had just reminded him of Lanie.

As he slipped the ring over the third finger on her left hand—to the accompaniment of enough flashbulbs to light a Vegas show—for some reason, Miles recalled what Lanie had said when they'd been walking through the park the day before, about not having any friends she might pull into a charade like this one. That meant she had no close, intimate friends. No one with whom she confided secrets. No one with whom to share things one only shared with those one trusted implicitly. The realization bothered him, but he decided to dwell on it later. Right now, they had a whirlwind romance to plan and carry out.

Oh, man, he couldn't believe he'd actually just put thought to the words *whirlwind romance*. It began to dawn on him then just what was going to be involved in this charade. That he was going to be viewed as a man so besotted with love that he'd willingly surrender his liberty, his life, his home, his tomcatting, his very identity, in order to shackle himself to one woman for the rest of his life. That he would have to make public appearances with Lanie and act the way men did when they were at the mercy of their feelings for a woman. That all the women out there he might meet and like to get to know better over the next couple of months would be completely off-limits to him. That his friends were going to look at him as a sellout, because if there was one thing Miles Fortune had sworn he would never do, it was get married.

As he gave Lanie a brief, chaste peck on the cheek for the photographers—no reason to risk losing control the way they had the night before—Miles wondered how he was supposed to survive this phony engagement with his manhood intact. Especially since, after this phony engagement, his manhood—among other things—was never going to be the same.

The days following the press conference passed in a blur for Lanie. For the sake of authenticating the engagement—not that it would ever be authentic, mind you—she and Miles were... Oh, *coerced* was probably too strong a word to use. Encouraged? They were *strongly* encouraged, she finally settled on, to attend a number of public functions that might promote the validity of their union. Luanne Meyers had naturally been filled in on all the particulars of the situation before Tom had spoken with Lanie and Miles, but, ever the dutiful first lady, she had supported her husband every step of the way. But where Lanie's father figured his work was done after the press conference, Lanie's mother knew her work was just beginning. Because Luanne, however involuntarily, had just stepped into the shoes of mother of the bride. What kind of mother would she be to let wedding plans, however small but now made public, go untended?

So now, in addition to stumping for her husband's gubernatorial campaign, Luanne Meyers also had a phony wedding to plan. To say Lanie felt a tad guilty for the added burden was an understatement.

Still, it wasn't as if Lanie's life was a barrel of armadillos at the moment, either. Nor was Miles's. What had started off as a scandal that might very well end the governor's bid for a second term blossomed over those following days into something that might very well secure his seat in the governor's mansion again. Because everybody loved a wedding. And a wedding in the governor's family meant a wedding for the state of Texas. Every time Lanie turned around, she was reading something about her upcoming nuptials and how exciting it would be to have a wedding for the daughter of a sitting governor. This when, mere days ago, many had been calling for Tom Meyers's head.

Only in America, Lanie thought as she read a headline in the *Dallas Tribune* on the day of the elections: Governor Goes On Glowing Over Goddess And Groom! Her dad had taken a lemon—Lanie's compromising position with Miles Fortune—and turned it not into something as pedestrian as lemonade, but into a gourmet lemon cream pie with frothy meringue. Or, even more appropriately, into a lavish, multitiered, lemon chiffon wedding cake with roses atop it.

But the days hadn't been entirely full of tension, Lanie had to concede. In fact, in many ways, this had been one of the best times of her life. Because she'd been able to spend so much of it with Miles. Not only had they attended a number of get-togethers in Austin, but they'd spent a full day at the Flying Aces, where she'd been able to meet more of his family. They'd been wary at first, and Violet, Lanie had sensed, had been downright suspicious. But she and Miles must have put on an Oscar-winning performance, because by day's end, the Fortune clan had been smiling and congratulatory and making Lanie promise she'd move to Red Rock after the wedding.

But that had only brought back the guilt of lying. Miles's family was just so nice and had ultimately been so kind and so welcoming to her. They truly believed the two of them would be getting married and more than once had hinted about the next generation. How long would they wait to start a family? Lanie had asked Miles on the drive back to Austin if they shouldn't be honest with his family, the way they had been with Lanie's mother. But he had assured her it was better this way, that there were too many Fortunes to leak the truth, however accidentally. He'd promised her it would be fine, that they'd all understand when the big breakup came after the first of the year.

Lanie hadn't been convinced, though, and she'd promised herself she'd do her best to keep her distance from the family so that there would be little chance of anyone coming to like her too much. She just didn't want to cause any more trouble than she already had, didn't want to add hurt feelings to what was already a painful situation. If that meant Miles's family thought her stuck up or cold, then so be it. It was better than having them grow attached to her—and her to them—and having to cut ties once she and Miles announced their breakup.

It was going to be hard enough, she thought, saying goodbye to Miles when the time came. He was just so wonderful, in so many ways. And after the way she had responded to that kiss in the park that day...

By mutual and unspoken agreement, neither of them had kissed like that again. In public, they held hands, kept their arms around each other, touched shoulders and elbows and backs. Occasionally, they'd indulged in a quick peck or hasty brush of their lips. But both remembered too well how easily they'd lost control that first time. No sense risking a repeat, Lanie had decided. And Miles evidently felt the same way, because he didn't push the matter, either.

But he really had been wonderful through everything. Any other man wouldn't even have agreed to go through with such a charade, turning over his entire life to a family he didn't even know—never mind that it was the first family of Texas. Any other man, if he had agreed to go along with it, would have expected some kind of compensation or remuneration in return. Any other man sure wouldn't have been as easygoing, even happy, about it as Miles was.

Miles had honestly been nice. And he'd been charming. And sweet. And attentive. To any casual observer, he really was in love with her and looking forward to spending the rest of his life with her.

Not that Lanie believed a bit of it. She knew Miles wasn't the sort of man to fall in love. And even if he had been, she wasn't the sort of woman men fell in love with. Oh, she knew men liked her, and she knew she was fun to be around. But falling in love? Building a life together? Happily ever after? That wasn't what men saw when they looked at Lanie Meyers. They saw good times. They saw fun. And that was the way Lanie wanted it to be. Right?

Right.

She no more wanted this to be a real engagement than Miles did. Even if there had been times over the past week when she'd almost forgotten they were both just playing a part. That was part of the fun. She was having a good time. No way was she starting to care about Miles in a way she'd never cared for another man. No way was she hoping for something more than a phony engagement. No way was she falling in love with him.

Because that wouldn't be like her at all.

By the time the polls closed on election day, Lanie was pretty sure she was strung more tightly than even her father was. All day long, the race had been, according to every local newscaster, "too close to call." In some precincts her father would squeak ahead of his opponent by a small margin. In others, he would be edged out by the tiniest percentage. Back and forth it went all day long, until all three Meyerses, not to mention everyone who'd worked on the campaign, were snapping and impatient and ready to commit mayhem.

Even Miles seemed stretched to the limit, Lanie saw when she caught his eye in the ballroom of the Ritz-Carlton, which the Meyers campaign workers had reserved almost a year ago for their victory celebration, when no one dared even think that Tom Meyers wouldn't win a second term in office. Of course, a year ago Tom Meyers's bid had been pretty secure. It hadn't been until the last few months that his opponent had come up so quickly in the polls. Surely, though, it would still be a victory celebration, Lanie thought as Miles smiled encouragingly at her. Her father couldn't lose after all they'd been through.

She realized then, though, that her anxiousness for her father to win had little to do with her father. No, it was more because if Tom Meyers *didn't* win, there would be no reason for Lanie and Miles to continue with their phony engagement. It wouldn't matter if they called it off tomorrow, since no one would be scrutinizing them anymore. Everyone would be looking at the new governor, waiting for him or a member of his family to be thrust into scandal. Lanie's scandal would be old news.

However, if her father did win, then she and Miles would still be in the spotlight, still be the subject of gossip and speculation and would still need to continue with their charade. At least for a couple more months, until all the hoo-ha surrounding the election died down, and her father's inauguration and policy-making claimed the focus again. Then she and Miles could gradually fade into the woodwork, and, ultimately, they could end both their engagement and the farce that had become their lives.

Still, Lanie thought, it hadn't felt like a farce the last couple of weeks. What it had felt was…good. Nice. Fun. She liked Miles. A lot. Probably more than she should. She'd liked being with him and talking to him and sharing her days with him.

And she'd liked touching him. Holding his hand. Looping her arm around his waist. Having his arm circling her shoulder. Kissing him, even if it was only for show and never overly passionate. Not like that first one at the park, when he'd nearly made her forget who and where she was.

Something hot and manic kindled in her midsection at the memory. Or maybe it was just looking at Miles that did that. He looked so handsome tonight, dressed for the occasion in a conservative dark blue suit, white dress shirt and burgundy silk tie. So all-American, she couldn't help thinking. He would totally fit with the rest of Lanie's family up there on the podium when the time came for her father's victory speech—because it *would* be a victory speech, she decided then. Her mother was dressed in navy blue, too, while Lanie, ever the bright spot, fashion-wise, had opted for a clingy bright red cashmere sweater dress. She'd toned it down with a discreet pearl necklace and earrings and bracelet, and flat red pumps. Still, she must not be too discreet, she thought with a smile, since Miles had scarcely taken his eyes off of her all evening. Of course, she'd rather been planning on that when she'd chosen her outfit.

She tried not to dwell on why. Because deep down, in spite of her admonitions to the contrary, she knew she was falling hard for Miles Fortune. And she was trying very hard to make him fall for her, too. It was pointless, she knew. He simply wasn't the sort of man to fall hard for a woman. Or, if he did, he didn't stay down long. As perfect as he looked here at the party to commemorate her father's political victory, Miles Fortune wasn't, at heart, a family-values kind of guy. It would serve Lanie to remember that. Funny, though, how she just kept forgetting.

"Quiet down, everybody! Quiet down!"

The thunderous voice of Dennis Stovall, her father's campaign manager and Miles's friend, suddenly boomed over the loudspeaker behind Lanie, and she flinched, throwing her hands over her ears. She saw Miles laugh when she did, then make his way to her from across the room where he'd been speaking to Dennis's very pregnant wife, Jenny.

"Dennis is smiling," she heard Miles say as she dropped her hands to her sides again, only to have him immediately capture one and thread his fingers through it, as if it were the most natural thing in the world to do. "Must be good news coming."

Looks like good news is already here, Lanie thought, looking at their entwined fingers. Then she remembered her father. Oh, right. Miles meant for *him.*

"Lanie, Miles," Dennis said into the mike, "y'all need to get up here with Tom and Luanne."

Lanie turned to look at Miles and grinned. "Definitely sounds like good news," she said.

"Then we better get up there," he replied, smiling as broadly as she.

She let Miles take the lead as they waded through the crowd to the podium, her fingers tightening on his—or did his tighten on hers?—as they climbed up the steps and took their place on the left side of Tom Meyers. Lanie smiled at her mother, who stood on his right, then at her dad, who took her free hand in his, something that created a four-person chain of the Meyerses and Miles Fortune. For some reason, the realization of that made Lanie feel kind of warm and fuzzy inside.

Dennis grinned at them all again, then held up a piece of paper and turned back to face the crowd. "It's official!" he shouted into the mike. "Ladies and gentlemen, it's my honor and privilege to announce that Tom Meyers will continue to be your governor for another four years!"

Whoops of delight and celebration roared up into the ballroom, not the least of which were Lanie's and Miles's.

"It was close," Dennis yelled over the mayhem, "but the governor's esteemed opponent has officially conceded the election. With ninety-nine percent of precincts reporting, Governor Tom Meyers is solidly in the lead by nearly ten percent of the vote. Congratulations, Governor!"

Lanie watched as her father pulled her mother into his arms and gave her a quick peck on the lips and a fierce bear hug. Then he turned to Lanie and kissed her cheek, as well, before giving Miles's hand a vigorous shake. All around them, red, white and blue balloons cascaded from the nets that had held them captive against the ceiling, and confetti sailed through the air in a star-spangled blizzard, sparkling amid the flashbulbs exploding on the ballroom floor. The band at the foot of the podium struck up "Deep in the Heart of Texas" and everyone in the ballroom joined in. Lanie didn't think she'd ever felt a surge of happiness quite like the one that went blitzing through her then.

Because that was when Miles pulled her into his arms and kissed her, the way he had that first time, as if he really meant it.

No, even better this time, she thought as his warm lips captured hers. Because where the first kiss had been filled with passion and need and hunger, this one was filled with warmth and desire and affection. It was perfectly appropriate for the occasion, and yet it made her feel utterly indecent inside because the things it made her want to do—

Her thoughts were interrupted by a barrage of flashing lights, and she turned to find that she and Miles were actually overshadowing her father in terms of a photo opportunity. Miles seemed to realize it, too, because he shrugged and gave her a matter-of-fact smile. Before she could turn away, however, he pulled her close once more and whispered into her ear, "Later." Then he eased away from her and went to congratulate her father and take the media attention back to the governor.

Amazing, Lanie thought as she watched him go. They weren't even married yet, and he was already getting into the flow of what it meant to be part of a political family. Too bad their engagement was fake. He'd be the perfect political son-in-law.

Unfortunately, the "later" Miles promised her never materialized. The victory celebration moved to the governor's mansion and continued well into the morning, and by the time the crowd dispersed, Lanie was nearly asleep on her feet. She walked Miles to the front door along with the rest of the stragglers to tell him goodnight. When he kissed her this time, it was another one of those innocent, for-everyone's-eyes quickies. But he did drape an arm over her shoulder and pull her close as he waited for everyone else to leave ahead of him.

Then, when they were alone, he turned to her with an

expression that was anything but happy. "I'm going to miss you the rest of the week," he said.

"Me, too," she told him.

"I wish I didn't have to go."

"I wish you didn't, either."

"But I'll see you at the party at Steven's this weekend, right?"

"Of course," Lanie told him. "It's not every day my father presents an award to a member of your family. In a way, this is almost like a prelude to our wedding. Especially since the planning of the party actually led to a different wedding."

Lanie smiled as she said it, thinking it was pretty great that things had turned out the way they had for Amy Burke-Sinclair, her father's events planner. When Amy had been assigned to organize the party for Ryan Fortune, no one had expected she herself would end up being a member of the Fortune family. But during the planning of the event, she and Miles's brother, Steven, had fallen in love. Now Steven's place was really Steven and Amy's place. And next weekend, for Ryan Fortune's party, it would be *the* place to be seen in Texas.

"I never thought about it, but you're right," Miles said. "It really will be like a prelude to our wedding."

Except, Lanie reminded herself, unlike Steven and Amy's, *their* wedding would never be taking place. Why did she keep forgetting that? But then, Miles seemed to be forgetting it, too.

He didn't seem to notice either of their gaffes, however, because he smiled. "Another one of those situations where you and I might have met, had we not met already," he told her, calling to mind to the conversation they'd had at the park that day, when Lanie had said it seemed like destiny that the two of them should get together.

"Hey, you're right," she agreed, smiling back. "Funny how that keeps happening."

He nodded. "Funny."

Then he kissed her again, not passionately, but with clear affection. Warmth seeped through Lanie as he did, and she found herself missing him already.

"If I could skip this trip to Albuquerque, I would," he told her as he pulled away, referring to the business trip he'd told her he'd planned long ago and couldn't change now.

"That's okay," she said. "We've been spending so much time together lately as it is. I don't want you to get tired of me."

"No chance of that," he assured her.

She didn't know what to say in response to that, so she said nothing. Only enjoyed the warm curl of pleasure that coiled in her belly at hearing him say it.

"I'll miss you," he said again. Strangely, he sounded as if he meant it.

"I'll miss you, too," she told him. Strangely, she really did mean it.

"I'll see you Saturday night, though," he told her. "I'll come by here and pick you up, and we can drive out to Steven's together."

She nodded. "That'll be great."

"It's gonna be a helluva party your dad is throwing," Miles said. "Steven's told me a little bit about it, and it sounds like half of Texas is going to be there."

"Yeah, well, Dad never does anything halfway," she said. "Besides, it's not like he did any of the organizing himself. Amy did all the work."

"Well, it sounds like Amy's giving a helluva party, then."

"In more ways than she ever anticipated," Lanie said, laughing. "Because now she's the hostess, too."

"Saturday night," Miles said again, before brushing his lips lightly over Lanie's one last time.

"Saturday night," she echoed.

Then he turned away to walk to his car, and Lanie stood in the doorway watching him. She noted the way the moonlight silvered his dark hair and gilded his strong body, how his shoulders were so broad and his waist so narrow, how his arms swung confidently at his sides and his long legs covered the distance so effortlessly. Poetry in motion, she thought.

She couldn't wait for Saturday night.

Eight

Ryan Fortune looked down at the crowd that had gathered to see him receive his award from the governor this evening and wished he could feel as sociable and festive as they obviously did. Barely an hour after beginning, the party was in full swing, but the merriment and laughter and congenial conversation was barely a blip on Ryan's radar.

He'd done his best to put on a good front, though, had greeted everyone as warmly as he could and had accepted their congratulations and good wishes with what he hoped was at least a genuine-looking smile. Already, though, he'd needed to retreat for a bit and get his bearings, to try to sort through the numerous and conflicting emotions that had been ricocheting in his head all day. Hell, not all day. For weeks now. Maybe months. So he'd grabbed a beer and made his way up the stairs, ostensibly to follow a group taking a house tour, then had slipped out of the bunch unnoticed to fade into the shadows of the second floor.

Now as he gazed down into the crowd, he did his best to put his troubling thoughts on hold. Steven's new house outside of Austin was awash in golden lighting for the party; the honey-paneled walls and floor of the living room seeming to almost glow in the amber light. Partygoers dressed in a riot of festive colors and sparkling jewelry ambled through open French doors on the far side of the room into and out of the cool night air outside. Virtually all of them held drinks, and many, Ryan noted, held hands. He smiled in spite of himself at that, marveling at how many of the young people mingling below him seemed to have hooked up lately, many of them permanently.

Hell, even the two detectives who were investigating Ryan as a suspect in Christopher Jamison's death had decided to tie the knot. Not that Ryan had anything to do with killing anybody, suspect or not. But try telling that to the Red Rock cops. Just because the dead man bore the Fortune birthmark, detectives Gabe Thunderhawk and Andrea Matthews were just so certain it must be a family member who had committed the crime. Though there had been times when Ryan wouldn't have put it past one Fortune wanting to murder another one, when all was said and done, they were now a loving, close-knit bunch who could no more harm one another than they could stop the sun from rising in the morning. Lately, what with all the love running around the family, he couldn't think of a soul who'd want to harm anyone.

So many of the younger Fortunes were engaged or married now, he reflected further, focusing on a happier subject matter and pushing thoughts of the investigation to the back of his brain. The youngest of the triplets had been the most recent to go, having just declared his intentions to marry. Ryan shook his head at that. Never in his life had he thought he'd see the day when Miles Fortune would tie the knot. That boy had just been too footloose and fancy-free. Of the three triplets, Miles had been the charmer, the one who didn't seem capable of limiting himself to one woman. But in a few months, he'd be saying "I do" to none other than the governor's daughter. That boy might some-day be the father to a president, Miles thought now, since everybody knew that politics ran in the blood. Might be kind of fun having a Fortune in the White House someday.

As if conjured by his thoughts, Miles and his fiancée Lanie Meyers strode into view, their arms wrapped around each other in a way that spoke volumes. Ryan shook his head. How had those two kept their relationship a secret for months? he wondered. It was so obvious, seeing the two of them together, how very much in love they were. Ryan had been as shocked as everyone else in the family when he'd heard about Miles's engagement. And like everyone else, he'd been so sure the boy was making a mistake, that he was just dazzled by a glamorous, beautiful woman and blinded by infatuation. But seeing him and Lanie together, it was clear that the two were devoted to each other, that they loved each other, deeply and passionately, the way two people should when they want to spend the rest of their lives together. The same way he and his wife loved each other, Ryan reckoned.

Lily, he thought again, searching the crowd for his wife and spying her immediately. She looked so pretty tonight. Prettier than Ryan had ever seen her looking. At fifty-nine, she was still long-limbed and voluptuous, her Apache and

Spanish heritage evident in her high cheekbones and those big, exotic dark eyes of hers. Tonight she was paying homage to her heritage in her attire, wearing a brightly embroidered, fringed shawl over a black dress, cinched at the waist with a belt of silver conchos. Her black hair was pulled back, and more silver winked in her ears in the form of oversize hoops. She was as breathtaking today, Ryan thought, as she had been as a girl. He'd loved her since he was a teenager, and her marriage to someone else and a dalliance with his brother hadn't changed that. Somehow, he'd always known if he was patient, fate would reward him with Lily.

Even now, though, after so many years and so much love shared, there were days when he woke up in the morning and looked over at her in the bed beside him and felt sure he must still be asleep dreaming, because he couldn't quite believe she was his. Still, he should have known they would wind up together at some point, should have had faith that everything would work out as well as it had. Or, at least, as well as it had until recently.

How was he going to tell her he was dying?

He sipped his beer and watched Lily cross the room to where the governor and his wife were talking to a small group of people. Normally, her smile was dazzling when she was out socializing like this. Normally, she felt totally comfortable flitting from group to group, could come into a conversation in the middle and feel right at home and have something to contribute. Normally, at parties like this, Lily shone. Tonight, though, as had been the case so frequently, Lily's mood seemed dark and withdrawn. Although she nodded courteously at the Meyerses, she barely exchanged a dozen words with them before moving to another group. There, Ryan noticed, she once again exchanged a few perfunctory greetings and excused herself. He watched as she disappeared into the kitchen, knowing she'd be no more outgoing in there than she had been anywhere else tonight.

She knew something was wrong, he thought. He'd realized that a long time ago. He'd begun sensing her withdrawal a couple of months ago, and it had only seemed to compound as the weeks had passed. She'd been especially distant for the past few weeks, and there had been days when she'd seemed so sad. There had even been times when Ryan had come upon her suddenly, and her eyes had been red-rimmed, her nose pink, as if she'd been crying. Whenever he'd asked her about it, she'd muttered something about her allergies kicking up, or having read something in the newspaper that made her sad. But Lily wasn't one for easy tears, and he'd never known her to be bothered by allergies. When he'd pressed her about it, she'd just shrugged it off, putting it down to age. But Ryan knew better.

He just wished he knew how much Lily knew.

He told himself she must just be picking up on his own feelings of fear and concern about his recent diagnosis with the brain tumor, that she couldn't know the specifics of his condition. Violet Fortune had promised she would keep Ryan's prognosis to herself for now, had agreed to wait until he himself made the announcement to his family about his tumor. That announcement was going to have to come soon, he knew, because he didn't have much time left.

Six months. That was what Violet had told him last month. Ryan had six months left to live. Even less now. How was he supposed to fit the rest of his life into six months, when he still had so much that he wanted to do?

He told himself he should have no regrets, that he'd lived his life in a way that would make any man proud. Why, tonight he was going to be honored for all the charitable work he'd performed over the years, which just went to prove he had made every day count, not just for himself, but for others, too. And in a way, knowing he was on a timeline now was better than what a lot of people had. Now that he had no choice but to accept that his time here on Earth was limited, he'd be sure not to squander it. He'd appreciate every last moment he had, would take none of them for granted.

It wasn't as if anyone knew the real length of his or her days. Ryan could step off the curb tomorrow and be hit by a bus and not even have the six months allotted him with his inoperable brain tumor. No one was guaranteed a long, full life on this planet. Knowing what he did, he could at least be sure to make the most of what he had.

But how was he going to tell Lily? How would he tell anyone in the family? And how was he going to manage the next six months, when all of them knew he didn't have much time left? He wanted to make his final days joyful and productive. How could he do that with the pall of sadness and regret that was certain to come over everyone who knew the truth?

A flash of color below caught his eye, and his gaze settled on Lily once again. Almost as if she'd sensed him looking at her, she glanced up then, right at the spot where Ryan had been so certain he would be out of view of everyone. But where normally she would have taken his breath away with the sparkle of her shine, tonight her dark brows knit together in anxiety. Instead of moving toward the stairs to join him, which was what she would usually do, she turned her back on him and began to walk away.

It was time, Ryan thought. Whatever was wrong, he had to make it right. He couldn't have his last months with Lily be filled with worry and caution and fear. Whatever was bothering her, he'd find out what it was, and together, they could deal with it. Then he'd tell her the truth about his condition and they could go from there.

Draining the last of the beer from the bottle, Ryan turned toward the stairs.

Fresh air. That was what Lily Fortune needed at the moment. Fresh air, and lots of it. Setting her untasted margarita on the tray of a passing waiter, she made her way toward the French doors at the other end of Steven Fortune's living room, excusing herself as graciously as she could from anyone who tried to engage her in conversation along the way. If she remembered correctly, there was a walkway behind the house that led to a pond, a quiet, secluded place where she could sort out her thoughts and feelings.

She couldn't stop thinking about what Melissa Wilkes had said about Ryan. How she had hinted strongly that Ryan was having an affair. Even worse than that was the memory of what Lily had seen with her own eyes.

She told herself it couldn't be true. Ryan couldn't possibly be unfaithful to her. Not after everything the two of them had been through together. Not after the obstacles they'd been forced to overcome in order to be married. But his behavior lately had been so strange. There was no question in Lily's mind that there was something going on she should know about. That there was something very important he was keeping from her. But could Ryan really be carrying on with another woman? Could he have fathered a child with that woman? Was it truly possible?

Lily stepped carefully along the path, the light fading now as she strayed farther from the house. The night air was chilly, so she wrapped her wool shawl more snugly around her shoulders. Her heels weren't high, but neither were they made for walking on rough stone and thick grass, so she took great care with how she stepped, which slowed her pace.

What difference did her pace make, though? she asked herself. It wasn't as if Ryan would follow her. He probably hadn't even noticed she'd left the party. He'd been too pre-occupied lately with other things to notice her much at all.

No, she immediately corrected herself. That wasn't fair. Ryan had been attentive and affectionate lately. Even more so than usual, really. But, of course, instead of appreciating his overtures and returning them, Lily had found herself suspecting he was only acting that way with her because he felt guilty for his infidelity.

Infidelity, she repeated to herself. Such a harmless-sounding word for such a heinous act. But what else was she supposed to think? Last month, when her fear that Ryan was keeping something from her had gotten the better of her, she'd followed him one afternoon. No, she wasn't proud of herself for doing it, for assuming the role of suspicious wife and lowering herself to such a profound level of mistrust. But she'd had to do something or the fear and uncertainty would have gnawed at her until she couldn't stand it anymore.

Lily had been so dismayed when her husband went to the front door of a strange house. And when the front door had been opened by a young woman who didn't look familiar at all, who had a young boy at her side, Lily's dismay had turned to real fear. She had watched, shocked, as her husband smiled with clear affection for the woman, then hugged the little boy with even more. Lily had known then that neither of them were casual acquaintances. She had forced herself to keep driving, though, not to stop and make a scene. But she hadn't been able to push out of her brain the image of her husband with that woman and child.

Could the woman be someone Ryan was seeing on the sly? Could the child be his? Lily hated herself for even thinking such a thing. But she couldn't get past his behavior of late and the odd way he'd been acting. She sensed the withdrawal, the preoccupation with something that didn't include her.

And then there was that Melissa Wilkes and all the little suggestive things she'd been telling Lily about her husband lately, saying—without really saying anything, mind you—that Ryan might be seeing someone else. Not that Lily for a moment trusted Melissa Wilkes. Or Melissa's husband, for that matter. Oh, the Wilkeses put up a good front and tried to make everyone think they were of good stock, but there was just something about those two, Lily thought. Something that left a bad taste in the mouth. Yes, Jason Wilkes might have Ryan's stamp of approval, and he might be doing well at Fortune TX, Ltd., and he and his wife might live in one of San Antonio's nicest communities, and they might dress well and act like the cream of society. But bad breeding always showed in little ways, and the Wilkeses definitely came from damaged stock. Not that Ryan would ever believe that, Lily knew. He doted on Jason Wilkes the way he would a wayward son.

She exhaled an exasperated breath and pushed thoughts of the Wilkeses away to focus on her path instead. She could hear the soft, lapping sound of the water now and knew she was near. The moon overhead cast down just enough illumination that, mixed with the distant lights of Steven's house, made the pond visible. A fluid sliver of the moon's reflection bisected the pond from nearly one side to the other, and the purling of the water soothed her rattled nerves some. She could hear the sound of frogs croaking and crickets chirping, and the brisk November breeze cooled the last of her anger. But with anger gone, there was room for sadness, and Lily was very nearly overcome by it. She wrapped her shawl more tightly around her shoulders, though whether it was against the cold night air or the chilliness of her thoughts, she couldn't have said.

"Lily."

She heard Ryan speak her name from somewhere in the darkness behind her, but told herself she must be hearing things. He hadn't had that uncertain, affectionate tone in his voice since they were newlyweds.

In spite of her misgivings, though, Lily slowly turned around, and there, silhouetted against the backdrop of the party, which seemed so very far away now, stood her husband. She said nothing, however, neither greeted him nor told him she wanted to be alone. Frankly, she wasn't sure what she wanted at the moment. In a way, she'd never loved him more than she did in that minute, fearing that she'd lose him. But in another way, she was furious with him and wanted to tell him to leave her alone. How could he risk losing what the two of them had? How could he treat their love so carelessly? How could he treat *her* so carelessly? How could he keep secrets from her?

"They'll miss you at the party," she said softly, knowing that much, at least, was true. "I imagine the governor is looking for you right now, so that he can give you your award."

"The award will wait," Ryan said, his voice as soft as hers as it sliced through the darkness. "This is a lot more important."

Lily swallowed against the lump that formed in her throat. There really was something wrong, she thought. And now, finally, she and Ryan would deal with it.

"What's more important?" she asked. Even as she put voice to the question, she dreaded hearing the answer.

Instead of replying, he took a few more steps forward, his boots whispering over the grass, momentarily disrupting the frog-and-cricket chorus. He didn't stop until barely a breath of air separated them. Then he lifted his hand and, after only a moment's hesitation, brushed the backs of his knuckles across her cheek. Her eyes fluttered closed as he completed the gesture, then opened again when he dropped his hand back to his side.

He was so handsome, she thought. He'd been handsome when they were kids, but maturity had brought with it a confidence and masculinity that made him even more so. Even at fifty-nine, he was still fit and strong, solid muscle thanks to years of ranch work. His hair was still dark, with scarcely a thread of silver to be seen, and his eyes were the color of rich dark chocolate, a remnant of his mother's Mexican heritage. Even after all these years, and even when she felt unsure of his love for her, he made Lily's pulse race, made the blood in her veins sizzle, filled her heart to overflowing. No matter what happened, no matter what he told her, she would always love him, she knew. She just wished she could be as certain of his love for her.

"Maybe you could answer that question yourself better than I could," he said.

She feigned puzzlement. "What do you mean?"

He lifted one shoulder and let it drop. "You look so sad tonight, Lily," he said. "You've looked sad for weeks. The sparkle's just gone right out of you lately. And for the life of me, I can't figure out why."

His words, spoken so quietly and with such confusion, had the opposite effect on her. Suddenly, she was filled with anger and absolute conviction. She saw her husband again in her mind's eye, standing outside a house where he was clearly expected by the young woman and child inside. She heard Melissa Wilkes's voice in her ear, saying such hurtful things, and Lily wanted, at last, to know what was going on.

"Why am I sad?" she asked, throwing his question back at him. "Well, how am I supposed to feel when my husband, the man I love more than myself, more than life, has decided I'm not enough for him?"

Ryan narrowed his eyes at her, his lips parting in obvious shock. But all he said was, "What?"

"You heard me," she replied testily. "I know all about her, Ryan."

He shook his head, and had she not known better, Lily would have honestly believed he had no idea what she was talking about. "Her?" he echoed. "Who? Who are you talking about?"

Lily swallowed hard and forced the words out. "The woman you've been having an affair with, Ryan. I know all about it. I know about *her*."

But still he only gazed at her incredulously, as if she'd lost her mind.

"Oh, please," she said. "Don't insult me by thinking you've put one over on me. I've been suspicious for months, and I found out for sure a few weeks ago when you went to meet her. Well, it didn't work. I saw you with her with my own eyes."

By now Ryan was shaking his head slowly, but still he said nothing to defend himself.

"And I know she has a child," Lily continued relentlessly, unable now to stop herself. It was as if a floodgate had opened inside her, and she couldn't control everything that was spilling through it. So many emotions and fears and worries that she'd kept pent up for too long came crashing down inside of her, and she had nowhere else to put them, so she just let them run free.

"I saw you," she said again when Ryan remained silent. "I...I followed you one day," she confessed. "And I saw you go to her house. I saw her answer the door and welcome you inside. I saw you smile at her. And I saw you hug her child. Please, tell me the child isn't yours," Lily hurried on, fighting tears now. "I don't think I could stand it if you'd been carrying on with her for that long. It's like a knife in the heart to think you've been seeing her at all."

And then she couldn't hold back the tears any longer. She dropped her head into her hands and wept freely, not caring now how foolish she must look and sound, caring only about getting at the truth. Only after the truth was finally acknowledged could she and Ryan begin to rebuild.

Because she knew in that moment that she didn't want to lose him. That she would do whatever she had to do to win him back, to keep him close, to spend the rest of her life with him. She loved him. More than she had ever loved anyone. And the thought of not having him in her life was unbearable.

She told him that as she wept, how she didn't want to lose him, how her life wouldn't be worth living without him in it, how she would die if anything happened to him, how empty and lost she would feel if he weren't with her. At some point, she felt his arms circle her shoulders, and she felt him pull her close. She went willingly, not caring that he had betrayed her, wanting only to be close to him again, physically and emotionally, the way they had been before. She'd hated it these past few months, being so uncertain about their marriage, wondering if he still loved her, fearing that she might lose him. She couldn't go on like that anymore. Whatever was wrong in their marriage, they had to fix it, because Lily couldn't live without Ryan.

"Oh, Lily," she heard him murmur. "Oh, I can't believe you've been thinking I would have an affair. That I could even want another woman when I have you. I waited my whole life for you, darlin'. Stood by wanting you when other men had you, never quite believing you'd someday be mine. And then, when I had you, when I knew you loved me, too…" He shook his head slowly. "I would never do anything to risk losing you. Oh, honey…"

He drew her closer then, wrapping his arms around her completely, holding her in a way that let her know he would never let her go, and in that moment Lily knew that she had indeed been foolish to doubt his love for her.

"But…then who was that woman?" she asked. "Why did you go to see her?"

Ryan expelled a long, weary breath and called himself every kind of fool. Why hadn't he just been honest with Lily from the beginning? he asked himself. Why had he tried to keep Linda Faraday and her son, Ricky, a secret? Naturally, he'd wanted to protect the two of them, and shield them at a time that was so precarious for both of them. But he should have known better than to try to keep the secret from Lily. He and his wife had always shared everything. She was the only true confidante he had. But he'd felt an obligation to his brother, Cameron, too, however well-deserved that obligation had been on Cameron's part. And he'd wanted to respect Linda's privacy, too, until the time was right. Now, though, Ryan realized he'd just made a big mess of everything.

"Honey, let's find a place to talk," he said. "This is kind of a long story."

He turned to look back at the house, where the party for which he was the guest of honor was still going strong, then down at his watch. The governor was supposed to announce the award in a little over thirty minutes. But, hell, this was way more important than any award. This was his life.

Or what was left of it.

The thought unrolled in his head before he could stop it. He couldn't tell Lily about the tumor now. Not after everything she'd just told him about her life not being worth living without him. And not with her having been thinking all this time that he was having an affair with another woman.

God, how could she have suspected him of such a thing? he wondered. But then he reminded himself how preoccupied about his health he'd been for the past few months. How withdrawn and uncommunicative. He recalled now all the times she'd asked him if something was wrong and how he'd always brushed her off without really answering, not wanting to tell her about his fears for his health. And if she'd followed him and seen what she had…

Well, hell. He supposed he couldn't exactly blame her. Fear had a way of getting out of hand when it went without answers or explanations. He probably would have been suspicious, too, and he probably would have concluded the same thing about her that she had about him, even knowing how much they loved each other. Funny the way love made people act and feel sometimes. Funny how something that made you feel so good one day could make you feel so miserable the next. Funny how it was such a double-edged sword that way.

"I should have told you about Linda a long time ago," Ryan said, tightening his hold on Lily when he felt her tense. "I'm not having an affair with her," he repeated quickly, as adamantly as he could. "But I do have a tie to her. And to her son."

He waited to see what Lily would say to that, but she only pulled far enough away from him that she could look into his face. Her expression was a silent question mark. But at least she wasn't angry.

"Her son is my nephew," Ryan said. "The boy's father is my brother, Cameron."

"Cameron," Lily repeated. "But he's been dead for ten years. That boy didn't look ten years old."

"He is ten," Ryan said. "Cameron fathered the boy just before he died. And the mother nearly died that night with him."

Now Lily began to shake her head. "I don't understand. I thought Cameron was alone that night."

"I wish he had been," Ryan said. "It would have made so many things easier for everyone."

He inhaled a deep breath and released it slowly, weaving his fingers through Lily's as he led her away from the pond and slowly back to the house. They could talk and walk at the same time, and make their way slowly back to the party. Most of the crowd had headed back inside now that the night was turning cooler and the party was becoming more festive. He and Lily could stay outside by the pool if need be, if he hadn't finished his story by then. They needed to get back before someone—namely the governor of Texas—came looking for them.

"Cameron was with a woman named Linda Faraday the night of the accident," Ryan told Lily as they walked along. "They'd been seeing each other romantically, and although Linda didn't know it at the time, she was pregnant with Cameron's child."

"How has this been kept a secret all this time?" Lily asked.

"Well, this is where truth gets stranger than fiction," Ryan told her. "Until a few months ago, Linda was in a semiconscious state."

"But the boy…"

"The boy was born while she was not aware of her surroundings. She came out of her twilight place after the accident to find herself weak and debilitated and ten years older, only to learn that the man she'd been involved with had been in the grave for a decade, and she had a son she'd never met before. Can you imagine what she's had to go through to get reacclimatized? I've been trying to help her when and where I can. The Armstrongs—"

"Her son is the boy the Armstrongs have been fostering all this time," Lily surmised, knowing that about the couple who were her and Ryan's close friends. "He's Ricky. I didn't recognize him that day I followed you. I was just so frantic seeing you with another woman…." Her voice trailed off, but she didn't sound angry or sad anymore, and for that Ryan was grateful.

He nodded. "The Armstrongs agreed to be his foster parents, and they've raised him like one of their own. Now, though, Linda's trying to get to know him and come to terms with motherhood this late in the game. But it's not been easy," Ryan said with much understatement.

Lily gazed at him in thoughtful silence for a moment, trying to digest all that he'd told her. "I can't imagine what that must be like," she said. "To be young and carefree and in love one day, and the next to wake up to a completely different reality. That poor woman." She looked at Ryan and smiled. "I'm glad she has you to help her, and I'm glad Ricky's had a chance to get to know his uncle. I just wish, Ryan, that you would have told me about this a long time ago."

"I wanted to," he said. "I just didn't know how. I wanted to protect the boy, and I didn't have Linda's permission, with her being in the state she was in. I just wasn't sure what to do or say to anyone." He wrapped his arm around her and pulled her close. "But I am sorry I didn't tell you. I should have learned a long time ago that anything that affects me affects you, too. We're one and the same, Lily. It will always be that way."

They stopped at the edge of Steven's yard and watched the party from a distance, and this time the laughter and the music didn't sound so hollow to Ryan. He had his Lily back, and she wasn't looking at him anymore with that sad face and that faraway, worried look in her eyes. He knew he was still keeping something from her, knew he still had to tell her about his tumor. But not tonight. Not yet. For the first time in months, things between them felt good again. For the first time in months, Lily was smiling, a genuinely happy smile. Later, he could tell her the rest.

"I'm glad you told me, Ryan," she said as she leaned into his embrace. "I'm glad that I know the whole truth about everything. Now I can stop worrying. Now I know everything's going to be okay."

Ryan closed his eyes as he pulled his wife into his arms and held her close. He did his best to battle the guilt that welled up inside him. But Lily's words kept circling in his head and refused to be quiet. She didn't know the whole truth. There was still plenty to worry about. And in the long run, it wasn't going to be okay at all.

Oh, Lily, he thought as he wrapped his arms around her and held her as close as he could. *How can I tell you I'm going to die?*

For an intellectual guy, Steven sure did know how to party, Miles thought as he spun Lanie around on the dance floor. Hooking up with a woman who planned parties for a living had definitely loosened up the guy. Miles couldn't remember the last time he'd had this much fun.

The dance floor in question was really Steven's living room, but since he and Amy had just moved into the house recently, they had deliberately held off on buying furniture for this room until after the party for Ryan. Amy had designated it the dance floor for the evening, and a small country-and-western combo had set up in one corner, with a scaled-down bar, complete with bartender, occupying the corner opposite. It was close quarters when more than a dozen couples wanted to dance, but Miles didn't mind. That only meant he had to pull Lanie closer and move more slowly against her. Call him crazy, but it was actually kind of a nice arrangement.

The governor had gone all out for the party, though, Miles saw, footing the bill for it, even if Amy had done all the actual planning. The house was decorated with red, white and blue streamers that hung from the ceiling, a huge Texas flag hanging over the podium where Ryan would soon be presented with his award. The wine and spirits had flowed freely, putting everyone in a festive mood—though some had become a little too festive, in Miles's opinion—and the food, though light appetizers, was plentiful. Semiformal attire had been specified on the invitations, so everyone was dressed to the nines, which meant that, for Texans, everyone took it well past tens. The crowd fairly glittered from sequins and gems.

Miles, though not glittering, had donned his best suit, and was making sure he steered clear of any plant life in the house. Lanie, however, was dazzling, wearing a snug, sparkly gold cocktail dress that hugged her luscious curves in a way that ensured his attention would be fixed on her all night. Hell, his body would doubtless be fixed on hers all night, too, since he wasn't about to let her out of his sight dressed like that for fear that some poacher might try to make time with his fiancée.

There it was again, he thought. He was thinking of Lanie in terms of his fiancée. His real fiancée, not his phony one. He'd been making that mistake a lot over the past few weeks.

Before he could think too much more about it, however, the band played the final notes of its selection, and Dennis Stovall took the stage to bring everyone's attention around and introduce the governor. The people who had trickled outside to mingle on the deck and patio returned to the house when they heard the announcement, making the already crowded room shrink even more.

There was a weird sort of energy in the air tonight that was unmistakable, Miles thought as he surveyed the crowd. Part of that, he knew, was simply the result of a huge group of people gathered in a small space. But there was something else, too, he decided, something that hummed and crackled and perplexed, something that brought with it both a tingle of excitement and a swell of tension. Some extraordinary, unfamiliar…*thing*, he thought, unable to find a better word for it. Something he was hard-pressed to explain or identify.

Telling himself it was just a result of his own strange feelings about what was happening between him and Lanie, Miles did his best to shrug it off and tried to pay attention to what was happening on the other side of the room. After the governor took the mike from Dennis and said a few words about himself—of course—he thanked everyone for coming and then turned to the man standing beside him: Ryan Fortune. Tom Meyers spoke at length about Ryan's recent work on the environment and his life-long volunteerism and charitable deeds, citing his work with a number of organizations. Then, on behalf of the people of Texas, he presented Ryan with the Hensley-Robinson Award, to the accompaniment of wild applause, cheering and whistling from the crowd.

Ryan was obviously moved by the distinction, because he kept his thanks, although eloquent and heartfelt, short. He'd never really been a man of few words, Miles thought of his distant cousin, whom he admired greatly. So the fact that he kept his speech brief this evening indicated how very honored he was by the governor's award.

The crowd applauded and whistled again when Ryan exited the stage. The governor said a few more words about Ryan, then, almost as an afterthought, mentioned his daughter's recent engagement and upcoming wedding. Miles waited for himself to become indignant, thinking Tom Meyers had overstepped his bounds by using an event like this to further his own agenda. Instead of indignation, however, Miles found himself feeling pleasure. Warmth. Satisfaction. Delight. Without even realizing what he was

doing, he wound an arm around Lanie's waist as everyone
in the room turned their attention to the recently engaged
couple to murmur their congratulations, and he was oddly
gratified when Lanie leaned into him as if it were the most
natural thing in the world for her to do. And then, as one,
they turned to each other and shared a quick kiss, as if that,
too, came naturally.

Then the governor was leaving the stage, and the
crowd's attention turned elsewhere. Miles and Lanie,
though, continued to stand with their arms looped around
each other's waists, neither, evidently, wanting to let the
other go just yet, even though they were firmly out of the
spotlight.

"Okay," Lanie said beside him as she surveyed the
crowd. "I know I'm not going to be tested on this, but
you're going to have to go over who all these people in your
family are for me again. There are just so many of you Fortunes. Now, Steven and Amy I know, obviously," she said,
nodding toward their hosts. She sighed with something
akin to wistfulness. "And, frankly, I would kill to have hair
like Amy's."

Miles noted the fall of strawberry blond hair on his
brother's wife and, although it was certainly pretty enough,
he preferred blond blondes. One in particular, he thought
further as he looked back at Lanie, who had left her hair
loose tonight for a change. He'd been itching to weave
it through his fingers all night and succumbed to the
temptation enough now that he lifted his hand from her
waist to duck it under her hair, curling his fingers around
her nape.

"And Steven I'll always recognize," Lanie said, her
voice sounding just a little more breathless than it had be-

fore Miles touched her, "since he looks just like you. It's funny, though, but I don't have any problem telling the two of you apart. And I can tell you from Clyde, too, even across a crowded room. But I can't tell Steven and Clyde apart to save my life."

"It's the dimple," Miles said. "That's how everybody tells me apart from them."

But Lanie shook her head. "No, it's not, actually. Even when you're not smiling, I can tell which one is you with no trouble at all."

That was a good sign, Miles thought. Until he wondered just what it was a good sign of—or why he was so happy.

"But as long as your brothers are with their wives," Lanie said, nodding this time toward Clyde and Jessica, "I'll know who's who." She emitted that yearning sound again. "But, frankly, I would kill to have a body like Jessica's," she added.

"Hey, that body is a part of Jessica's work," Miles pointed out about his brother's model fiancée. "She's worked hard to look like that. For some people," he added, turning to look back at Lanie again, "that great-looking business just comes naturally." He gave her an affectionate squeeze. "Besides, I don't know what you're complaining about. Your body's perfect."

He wasn't sure, but he thought she blushed at that. Honestly, Miles had no idea what had made him say what he did. It wasn't as if he was intimately acquainted with her body. Well, not the way he wanted to be. Not the way he'd been dreaming about lately. Too often and too much. Yeah, it really was a shame this wasn't a real engagement, he found himself thinking. Then again, no one had said he and Lanie couldn't enjoy the benefits of an engagement without actually being engaged. The way she'd been looking at him tonight made him wonder if she'd been thinking the same thing.

In a word, *hmm*.

"And that's Violet and Peter," Lanie said, pointing at Miles's sister and brother-in-law-to-be, whom she had also met previously. "Two neurologists. That's going to be an interesting marriage."

And not just because they were both neurologists, either, Miles couldn't help thinking. Peter Clark and his sister were both so bent on helping other people, he just hoped they didn't forget to enjoy each other from time to time. Not to mention Celeste, the little girl they were in the process of adopting. Then again, he thought as he saw Peter steal a kiss from Violet, that probably wasn't going to be a problem.

"And, of course, I know Daniel Fortune from his work with the D.A.'s office," Lanie said, directing her gaze now at Miles's tall, athletically built cousin. She leaned closer and added conspiratorially, "Just between you and me, I think Dad's grooming him for big things. I predict a big political future for him." Then she held up her finger to her lips in a don't-tell-anyone gesture that made Miles want to kiss her.

Oh, hell, whom was he kidding? Just watching her walk across a room made him want to kiss her.

"But I'm not sure about the rest," she said. "Who am I missing?"

Miles looked around the room. "Well, let's see. Over there is my cousin Susan Fortune," he said, pointing at his petite, tawny-haired cousin. "She's Daniel's sister. A psychologist who works with troubled teenagers. She's talking to her sister Kyra," he added, referring to the taller,

platinum blonde at Susan's side, "who's an executive for
Voltage Energy Company. Their brother is Vincent," he
added, directing Lanie's attention now to a very large,
dark-haired man not far from Susan. "He's the oldest of the
four. But all of them had a rough time of it growing up. It's
amazing, really, that they all turned out as well as they did.
Their parents weren't exactly mother and father of the
year. Vincent was sort of the guiding hand in that family."

"What's he do for a living now?" Lanie asked.

"He owns a security business," Miles told her. "And he
works as a bodyguard."

"No kidding?" she said. "That's interesting."

"Over on this side of the room," Miles continued, directing Lanie's attention toward another of his cousins, "is
Logan Fortune, who's the CEO of Fortune TX, Ltd. and
that's his wife, Emily, with him. They're talking to the
guest of honor, whom you also know by now."

"Ryan Fortune," Lanie said. "Of course I know him.
And his wife, Lily," she said, correctly identifying the
darkly beautiful woman at Ryan's side. "They seem so
perfect for each other."

Miles nodded. "They are. Went through a lot to be together, but finally made it. I can't see anything ever coming between those two."

He pointed out a few other family members and friends,
filling Lanie in on the basics. The crowd was enormous,
though, and there were more than a few people present at
the party that even Miles didn't know.

"I'm just sorry my parents couldn't be here tonight," he
said as he concluded his inventory. "They're so excited
about us and can't wait to meet you, but they had to be in
Washington, D.C., this weekend for a summit that the vice-

president himself invited them to participate in six months ago. They just couldn't miss it. But they're already planning an engagement party for us in New York, so they can show off the newest family member to all their friends."

When Lanie's head snapped around to look at him and he saw the look in her eyes, Miles realized just how seriously everyone was taking this phony engagement. He and Lanie both were obviously feeling guilty about misleading so many nice people. But what was the alternative? To really get married?

And why, Miles wondered, did such an option not make him want to scream in horror, the way it should? This whole thing with Lanie was supposed to be a farce. Playacting. Pretend. But at some point over the last few weeks, it had begun to feel strangely real. What was especially bizarre, though, was that he kind of liked the feeling of reality his engagement to her had taken on.

"Everything will be fine," he said in response to her unspoken panic. "I promise."

Lanie smiled, and a funny little ripple of pleasure wound through him, and he tightened the arm he'd wrapped around her waist. When the music started up again, he drew her into his arms and danced her out to the middle of the floor. As he pulled her close and curled an arm around her waist, he lowered his head to her ear and nuzzled it. Very softly, very affectionately, told her, "Oh, and by the way, sweetheart. You are going to be tested later on which Fortune is which. I hope you were paying attention."

Nine

Melissa Wilkes was watching very closely as Ryan Fortune made the circuit of the party, because she was so mad at herself for having missed seeing him slip outside earlier. That wasn't like her at all. She never lost sight of a man once she set her sights on him, as evidenced by her having wrapped her so-called husband, Jason, so soundly around her little finger a long time ago. But she'd had a few drinks since arriving at the party, so maybe her edge was a little fuzzy. In any case, she was keeping an eagle eye on Ryan now, so she saw him when he looped his arm soundly around Lily and pulled her close, and she saw Lily smile affectionately at him in return.

Well, shoot. They weren't even supposed to have come back in from outside together, let alone be looking all lovey-dovey like that now. What on earth had happened outside earlier? she wondered. Lily Fortune was supposed to be convinced her husband was having an affair, and Ryan was supposed to be turning his attentions toward Melissa and becoming completely besotted with her.

Oh, all right, so maybe she had a long way to go before reeling in Ryan Fortune. He did seem to be more smitten with his wife than most men were. Go figure. But that had never been a problem for her before, she thought smugly as she lifted a hand to the platinum blond hair that had once been mousy brown. She was the sort of woman every man wanted and no man could resist, with the face of an angel and a body made for sin. She'd have Ryan Fortune dancing to her tune soon enough—a sultry, sexy tango, too. She was just going to have to work harder, that was all.

And she was going to have to make sure Jason was occupied elsewhere when she went to work.

Her full, heavily lipsticked mouth flattened into a tight line as she watched Ryan and Lily Fortune cross the room to where the governor and his wife were standing. Then she shifted her weight onto one spike heel and planted a hand on one curvy hip clad in skintight red spandex that stopped high above the knees and scooped low above her ample breasts. She'd accessorized the heart-stopping dress with huge crystal chandelier earrings and a dazzling rhinestone necklace, for all the good it had done. Although she was certainly turning heads this evening—even the governor had given her a twice-over—she might as well have been invisible to Ryan Fortune.

Well, this was a fine howdy-do, Melissa thought bitterly. After all the trouble she'd gone to for the past few months to drive a wedge between Ryan and Lily Fortune, suddenly they looked as if they were more in love than ever. Now what was she supposed to do?

She looked at her empty glass. Have another Cosmopolitan for starters, she figured. When the going got tough, the tough got a drink. That was one of the few actually useful things she'd learned from her mother. She took a minute to balance herself on her sky-high heels, then teetered precariously over to the bar. The combo in the corner had segued from a lively country tune to an old Hank Williams standard, so Melissa slowed her own pace to keep time. That would enable her to throw a little more swing into her hips, too, something that was bound to turn heads. Maybe even Ryan Fortune's, if she did it right.

Jason Wilkes—who'd been Jason Jamison in another life—watched his pretend wife, Melissa, as she wiggled her way over to the bar. His wife, he repeated distastefully. Right. She was about as much a wife to him as an armadillo would be. Hell, worse. At least an armadillo made a tasty entrée. And you wouldn't wind up on death row for killing one of those.

Not that that was going to stop Jason from killing Melissa.

Hell, he could do that without getting caught. Because Melissa—bless her stupid little conniving heart—had managed to set herself up for murder in a way that would bring attention to countless other people before Jason. All he had to do was make sure he had an ironclad alibi when he completed the task—which he would, because for once in his life, he'd formed his plan up to the very end before attempting to execute it.

His mouth curled up at the unintentional pun. Yeah, Melissa's days were numbered. And that number was dwindling fast. In a matter of days, her body would be washing ashore in Lake Mondo, right near where Jason had dumped his brother Christopher over five months ago. They still didn't suspect him for that one, either. Although it had surprised, and delighted, Jason that Ryan Fortune was a prime suspect in Christopher's murder, he intended to take full advantage of the fact. He was going to make sure the man was a prime suspect in Melissa's death, too.

Oh, yeah. Jason had it all planned. Now all he had to do was keep Melissa from drawing too much attention to herself before he had a chance to kill her. Which wasn't going to be easy, he knew. Especially at a party like this, where she'd gone out of her way to cultivate an audience.

Sure enough, virtually every eye in the room was on Melissa as she stood at the bar, slugging back the last of one of those pink drinks she liked so much. He could tell by the way she slammed the glass back down onto the bar—nearly tumbling off of her shoes as she did—that it wasn't the first one she'd enjoyed that night. Not by a long shot. His suspicion was only confirmed when she sidled up close to the man standing beside her and threaded her fingers through his hair, pressing her lush body fully against him.

And it wasn't even Ryan Fortune. It was one of the waiters, filling a tray with drinks. Jeez, the woman really didn't care who she threw herself at. What the hell good was a waiter? Those guys were at the bottom of the food chain. Even Jason had never worked as a waiter in his sorry life.

Enough was enough. Jason strode forcefully over to where his "wife" was still trying to wrap herself around the clearly uncomfortable young man, grabbed her by the wrist and spun her around. Belatedly, he realized how his actions must look to everyone who was watching—which was everyone in the room. So he did his best to loosen his hold on her, and he kept his voice low as he hissed, "For God's sake, Melissa, how much have you had to drink tonight?"

She was obviously not happy to have had her attentions to the waiter interrupted. Jason looked past her now and saw that the man was really a kid. Probably not even out of high school. Melissa had sunk to a new low by coming on to him.

"Not enough," she spat back at Jason. "Because you're still here. And you're still ugly." She must have thought that was hysterical, because she burst into raucous, drunken laughter.

Unable to help himself, Jason clenched his fingers more tightly on her wrist, but somehow he forced himself to stay calm.

"Ease up on that stuff, honey," he said through clenched teeth, "or I'll wring your pretty little neck."

She jerked her hand free of his and tossed her hair back over her shoulders, turning away from him at the same time. "That's about all you can do to my pretty little neck lately," she said. "You're not half the man Ryan Fortune is."

Being compared to any Fortune made Jason seethe with anger. He was better than all of the Fortunes put together. But who'd been rewarded with the money and the land and the prosperity and the careers and the social standing and the good fortune? he asked himself bitterly. Not him. Not Jason Jamison. No one from the Jamisons had done well, thanks to the Fortunes hogging all the wealth and windfalls. Everything had gone to that side of the family.

And not one of them deserved it. They were no better than Jason. On the contrary. He was smarter and harder working, stronger and better-looking. In every possible way Jason was better than every last person bearing the Fortune name. He'd had to work to get where he was. And beg, struggle, fight and plan. But he'd made it. On his own blood, sweat and tears, he'd climbed as high as any of the rest of them. And by God, he'd climb higher still. He wasn't about to risk losing any of it. Not when he was so close to having it all.

He looked at Melissa again and marveled that he could ever have loved her. Because now...

Love and hate, he recalled hearing, were separated by a thin line. Well, he'd crossed that line. The last thing he needed at this point was someone like Melissa who, with one misplaced word or action, could bring him down. Could pull him back into the filth and mire that had spawned him. No way was Jason going back to that. No way would he let Melissa send him there. What little use he'd had for her was gone.

She turned to look at him again, sneering over the rim of her glass. "Why don't you just go on home, Jason, and let me have a good time for once in my life?" she asked. She curled her lip in contempt as she added, "You don't belong at this party anyway."

It was the worst possible thing she could have said to him, telling him he wasn't good enough to mingle with the Fortunes. And it was just the thing to send him right over the edge.

"You've had enough, Melissa," he told her. "On the contrary, it's time for *you* to go."

And after we leave, he added to himself, *once we're*

clear of the house where it's dark and secluded, I'll tear you limb from limb with my bare hands. And then I'll feed you to the fish in Lake Mondo.

"You think I've had enough to drink?" she echoed, blinking her blue eyes in mock innocence. "Well, all right then, Jason. Why don't you finish this one for me?"

Before he realized her intention, she threw the fresh drink the bartender had set in front of her in Jason's face and slammed the empty glass back onto the bar.

He barely registered the collective gasp that went up around him, because all he could see at that moment was red. He forgot what happened when he let his anger get the best of him, forgot how when he lost control he got into trouble.

He reached for a napkin to wipe his face as he watched her walk away, and he vowed that it was the last time Melissa would ever cause him problems. This time he really was going to wring her pretty little neck, he told himself. Quite literally.

And quite fatally.

Natalie McCabe was getting bored. She was a hard-nosed newshound, not a society columnist, and parties like the one Steven Fortune was hosting for his cousin Ryan just weren't the kind of thing that normally made it onto her journalistic radar. She would have been much more comfortable wearing a suit than a simple black cocktail dress. The only reason she'd agreed to cover the affair was because the governor was attending, and that did give the evening some passing resemblance to a current event.

Still, if Joe Franklin, her editor at the *San Antonio*

Express-News, had his way, she'd be relegated to the hors d'oeuvre patrol for the rest of her career, covering canapés and coiffures. But Natalie was determined to keep her journalistic integrity intact. She'd show that good ol' boy at the big news desk what for. She wouldn't mention a single appetizer in her entire story.

Take that, Joe.

She was just glad Tom Meyers had finally presented Ryan Fortune with his do-gooder award. Now that she'd taken the requisite photographs and jotted down enough quotes for her story, she could turn her attention to someone who held even more appeal to her than the governor and Ryan Fortune combined.

Jason Wilkes.

Natalie had figured there would be some representatives of Fortune TX, Ltd. at the party, since Ryan Fortune held a position of adviser to the company. She'd made it a point to recognize everyone in the higher echelons of the corporation. She was working on another story about Ryan's position there, and she'd hoped to get a quote from one or more of the high-ranking executives about how his work was affecting and shaping the company. Jason Wilkes would be an especially nice subject for an interview, since word had it that he was Ryan Fortune's protégé.

She'd done her best to go through the proper channels to meet with someone highly placed, but no one at the company would give her the time of day. Good-ol'-boy networks weren't just for newspapers, after all. Because of Natalie's gender and her age—and she looked even younger than her twenty-nine years, she knew—no one seemed to take her requests for an interview seriously. Or maybe it was just that the muckety-mucks of Fortune TX,

Ltd. were tight-lipped about everything to everyone, no matter who came asking for a quote.

In any event, she wasn't the sort of person to take no for an answer. And if Jason Wilkes was at a party she happened to be attending herself, she was smart enough and bold enough to take advantage.

So where was he now? she wondered as she scanned the big living room of Steven Fortune's home. She'd seen him earlier talking to a brassy blonde who was squeezed more tightly into her dress than toothpaste into a tube, a woman Natalie had overheard someone say was his wife.

She found Jason at the bar, tossing back what looked like a bourbon straight up. Double, if she wasn't mistaken. That must have been some conversation he'd had with the Mrs.

Natalie watched as he settled the empty glass back onto the bar. She waited until Wilkes passed through the door before following him, wanting to make sure she got him alone when she interviewed him. People always responded more frankly if there was no one else listening in on the conversation.

Peering around the door through which Wilkes had exited, Natalie was delighted to see him ascending the stairs to the second floor, where there were considerably fewer partygoers to contend with. She waited until his foot hit the top step before following, then kept an eye on him as he made his way down the long hall toward what she had discovered on an earlier tour of the house was a well-stocked library. She'd always heard that Steven Fortune was the smart one of the Fortune triplets.

Natalie's foot hit the top step just as Jason Wilkes disappeared into the library and pushed the door closed behind him. She frowned. She didn't want to intrude if he was meeting someone in there. Still, the door wasn't quite closed, so she figured whatever was going on in there couldn't be too private. As she drew nearer, though, she heard voices, and if she wasn't mistaken, they didn't sound too happy. In fact, they sounded angry. Her nose for news got the better of her, and she kept walking, slowly and carefully, until she could peek through the three-inch opening between the door and the jamb.

During those last few steps, she realized Wilkes was arguing with his wife, because she heard them exchange names, along with a few choice insults. By the time she reached the door and peeked through it, the argument had stopped, and the pair seemed to be embracing. Apparently they were as quick to make up as they were to fight with each other. Still, whatever was going on, it wasn't something Natalie needed to be witness to. She'd just try and talk to Wilkes later in the evening.

Silently, hastily, Natalie retreated down the hall. But something made her stop, a weird sound that just didn't quite seem…human. Or, if it was human, there was something horribly wrong about it.

Something sick and icy slid into Natalie's stomach, and the hairs on the back of her neck leapt to attention. She wasn't even conscious of turning around and walking back to the library door. Her heart pounded harder with every step she took, her palms grew damp and her mouth went desert-dry. She was lifting a hand to knock gently on the door—though why she would knock when she was nearly overcome with terror—when a loud thump made her entire body flinch and her heart very nearly stop beating.

Oh, God, she thought.

Not sure where she found the strength or presence of mind to do it, she gazed through the opening between door and jamb. She only saw one person—Jason Wilkes. He was closer to her now than he had been before, and instead of being in profile, his back was turned to her completely. His wife, however, was nowhere to be seen.

Until Natalie took another step forward that brought her within a hairbreadth of the door itself.

That was when she saw the blonde lying on the floor in a twisted heap, her body turned away from Natalie, but her face, eyes grotesquely wide, in clear view. Jason Wilkes had twisted her slender neck so hard with his beefy fists that he'd snapped it in two. His wife was dead, murdered by her husband's hand.

"Good riddance," she heard him say in a voice that dripped with contempt. "You were more trouble than you were worth."

Unable to help herself, Natalie cried out at the terrible scene. Not loudly, but loud enough that Jason Wilkes heard her and spun around to see her.

His eyes widened when he saw her standing there, but for one strange, terrible moment, neither of them moved or spoke. Then, in a voice more chilling than the one he'd used to address his dead wife, Wilkes said, "Take a good look, honey. Because you're next."

And then he lurched forward, toward the open door where Natalie stood in speechless, immobile horror.

She didn't remain speechless or immobile for long. Before Jason Wilkes had completed two steps, she was half-way down the hall. She nearly stumbled as she raced down the stairs in her low heels, grabbing hold of the banister just when she would have spilled face-first into the crowd below. Blindly, she pushed past faceless people, her attention fixed entirely on the front door.

Escape. That was all she could think about in that moment. Run away. Get away. Flee the premises before Jason Wilkes wrapped his fingers around her throat, too.

She tripped and slipped and skidded more than she ran to her car outside, grateful for her usual habit of parking her own vehicle in a place where it would be unobstructed. Still not thinking, still only reacting, she thrust the key into the ignition and ground it to life. Then, with a sputter of gravel and a squeal of her tires, she was tearing away from Steven Fortune's and toward blissful safety.

She was barely a mile down the road when some semblance of coherent thought returned. The first thing Natalie realized was that she wasn't running toward safety at all. Jason Wilkes had gotten a good look at her. He probably knew who she was, thanks to her efforts to talk to the people at Fortune TX, Ltd.

He'd come looking for her, she realized then. He was probably looking for her right now. It wouldn't take him long to discover she'd left, seeing as how her exit hadn't exactly been graceful. He might be starting his own car this very instant. Might be right behind her. Might catch up any second. Even if he didn't, he could find her. She was anything *but* safe right now.

She had to go back, she told herself. She had to go back to the party and tell them what had happened. Only when the man was behind bars would Natalie be safe again.

Without a second thought, she swung her car around in a vicious U-turn and headed back the way she had come. She kept an eye out for oncoming vehicles, just in case Wilkes had followed her. But she encountered no one on the short trip back, so she knew he must still be at the party, probably looking for her.

Swallowing her fear, she parked where she had before and hurried back to the house, constantly surveying her surroundings for a big, masculine shadow that resembled Jason Wilkes. But plenty of people were still milling about outside, and nothing looked out of the ordinary. The party was still in full swing when she entered the house, so she knew no one had found the murdered woman. She scanned the crowd quickly to see if Wilkes was in sight, but there was no sign of him.

Her host, she decided. She had to tell Steven Fortune what had happened. Calmly and coolly, so that no one would be spooked. When she found him he was talking to two other men who looked exactly like him. Natalie inhaled a deep breath and held it, hoping it might steady her rapid-fire pulse. Then, still scanning the crowd for signs of the murderer, she slowly made her way to the group of men.

"Which one of you is Steven?" she asked.

All three chuckled, but one replied, "I'm Steven."

Natalie nodded. How best to tell a man someone had just been murdered in his home? Finally, she just told him, "There's been a murder."

He looked at her blankly, as did his companions. "I beg your pardon?"

"There's been a murder," Natalie repeated evenly. "Upstairs in the library. Jason Wilkes murdered his wife. I saw it happen. You have to call the police!"

Before Steven could react, a woman approached them.

"The police are here," she said, breaking away from the crowd where she was partying. A man was behind her, both of them striding toward Natalie.

"What's this about a dead woman?" the man asked.

Natalie filled in the details. "And Wilkes saw me. But he's probably halfway to Tucson by now."

The police officers, who by now had produced their badges, nodded toward each other, then broke apart, the woman moving toward the stairs and the man moving toward the back of the house in practiced choreography.

"Call nine-one-one," the woman said as she ascended. "Give them this address. Tell them what's happened, and tell them there are two detectives on the scene—Andrea Matthews and Gabe Thunderhawk. But we need backup."

Immediately, one of the triplets broke from the crowd to follow her orders.

"Stay put," Andrea said when she saw Natalie start to follow her.

Although she balked at missing out on what would be the story of the evening, Natalie did as the detective told her to. She'd still give herself the exclusive on the story, she knew. But right now, it was more important to stay alive long enough to tell that story.

The next few minutes seemed interminable to Natalie, passing with agonizing slowness—and silence. She couldn't believe how quiet the house had become. All night, she'd been surrounded by music and laughter and the clinking of glasses and silverware. Now, though, no one was making a sound. Finally the detective appeared at the top of the stairs again.

"There's definitely a dead woman up here," she said. "No sign of the killer, though," Andrea said as she descended. "You said you saw him?" she asked Natalie.

Natalie nodded vigorously. "Yes. It was Jason Wilkes. He works for Fortune TX, Ltd. I was hoping to get an interview with him about a story I'm working on when I saw him arguing with his wife. Then, before I realized what was happening, he killed her."

"We'll need a statement from you," the detective said. "Don't go anywhere." To the two remaining triplets, she added, "No one is to go upstairs until I say it's all right." She looked at Natalie, then back at the Fortunes. "No one," she reiterated.

Then she took off in the direction her partner had taken, out the French doors and into the dark night. After that the silence in the house turned into a low, steady buzz, as everyone present digested the reality of the evening.

"Are you okay?" the remaining triplet who wasn't Steven said.

"I'm fine," she replied coolly.

She was about to say more, but the man was joined then by the governor's daughter, Lanie, who slipped her arm around his waist as he draped an arm over her shoulder. He was Miles Fortune, Natalie realized. The governor's son-in-law-to-be. Clyde, she realized, had been the one to go call the authorities.

She was thinking that maybe she'd break her own rule about never drinking at these functions when shouting from outside silenced the room again. But only for a few seconds. Then there was a single gunshot, followed by a number of outbursts from the guests. After a few more moments, the two detectives came spilling through the French doors again, this time with a struggling and hand-cuffed Jason Wilkes between them.

"Natalie McCabe," he said as the detectives pushed him past her, his dark eyes fastened intently on hers.

So he had recognized her after all, Natalie thought, nausea roiling through her stomach at the realization.

"Yeah, honey, I know your name," he added hatefully. "And I know where you work."

"Shut up," Andrea Matthews told him, shoving him toward the front door.

But Wilkes ignored the warning. "You watch your back, Natalie McCabe," he called out over his shoulder in just about the coldest, most malicious voice Natalie had ever heard. "'Cause I know where you live, too."

As Natalie watched the detectives close ranks around the killer, the shiver that went down her spine was nothing short of arctic.

Ten

Lanie blinked in surprise as Miles switched off the ignition and extended a hand across the car to drape it over her shoulder. She honestly couldn't remember a single part of the drive after they had left Steven's ranch, and she was surprised to see that Miles had driven her not to the governor's mansion, but to his hotel. She was astonished that she hadn't been paying attention. Her head had been too full of memories of what had happened, of how Jason Wilkes had looked as they'd carted him off in handcuffs, how he'd gazed so icily at that poor Natalie woman and so lethally threatened her.

"You okay?" Miles asked, his voice sounding as if it were coming through layers of cotton stuffing.

Although she didn't feel okay at all, Lanie nodded. "I think so," she said. "I just can't stop thinking about—"

"I know," Miles said, cutting her off before she could

even put voice to the events of the evening. It wasn't necessary after all.

"Why did you drive here?"

He shrugged. "Your parents were still being questioned, and it looked like they were going to be a while. Your dad told me he was planning to stay as long as the detectives did. I didn't think you'd want to go home and be all by yourself."

"You were right," Lanie agreed, touched by his concern. "Thanks."

She told herself it should feel awkward going to Miles's hotel room. Strangely, it didn't feel awkward at all. He'd adopted the habit of reserving a suite whenever he visited Austin, so there would be plenty of room for both of them. Not that she felt like sleeping tonight, she thought again. Still, she was happy she wouldn't have to spend the night alone.

"Let's go up, and I'll fix you a drink. I think we could both use one, actually. It's been a helluva night."

Lanie certainly couldn't disagree with that. When she and Miles had left the party, Steven and Amy were still being questioned by the detectives, as were a number of other partygoers, including Ryan Fortune himself. Lanie and Miles had been obligated to answer some questions, too, but since neither of them knew the Wilkeses or had witnessed any sort of incriminating behavior that evening, the police had let them leave. In spite of being far removed from the events, however, Lanie still didn't feel in any way comfortable.

"I'm not sure I'll be able to sleep tonight," she said.

"That makes two of us," Miles told her. "Maybe there'll be something on one of the cable channels we can watch. Or we could just order room service and play Nintendo."

He smiled at that, letting her know he was kidding, and some of Lanie's tension eased. Besides, playing Nintendo sounded kind of fun. She was pretty good at Super Smash Bros.

"Food sounds good, too," she said. "And definitely a drink," she added, letting him know that a nightcap was in order.

But when they arrived in his suite and Miles went directly to the desk to pluck the room service menu out of the collection of hotel information, the realization that he'd been thinking of food and nothing else didn't quite sit well with Lanie. In spite of that, she moved to where he'd taken a seat on the bed and looked over his shoulder at the selections. They agreed on a few appetizers, and Miles added a bottle of wine to the order when he called. As he spoke on the phone, Lanie rose from the bed and moved into the adjoining sitting room, telling herself it was *not* because the bedroom held any sort of significance but because there was more space in the other room. Not to mention the Nintendo.

When Miles joined her, he was loosening the necktie at his throat and unfastening the top two buttons of his shirt. Lanie swallowed hard as she watched the action, but he didn't go any further, only unbuttoned his cuffs and rolled them back and slipped off his shoes. She kicked off her high heels, as well, tucking her feet up under her on the sofa, then lifted the remote and switched on the TV.

A news report about the murder came on and she immediately turned the television off.

"No, turn it back on," Miles said. "I want to see if there's anything new."

Reluctantly, Lanie did as he asked, but she found herself drawn into the story, too. But they learned nothing new. As the reporter segued into another story, a knock sounded at the door. After signing for the room service order and tipping the waiter who had delivered it, Miles collapsed onto the sofa beside Lanie.

"So," he said, "what do you want to do?"

The reply that rose most quickly and completely in Lanie's head was in no way appropriate, because it featured her and Miles doing something together that she'd tried desperately not to think about but couldn't get out of her mind. Namely, get naked and horizontal.

So she hastily thumbed the remote again and quickly went right to the television's main menu.

"Movie," she said. "I think we should find a nice, funny romantic comedy to take our minds off of what happened tonight."

"Sounds good," Miles said.

But Lanie was so frazzled by the explicit thoughts still parading through her head that she rushed through the menu options and didn't pay attention to what she was selecting. Still, it looked like it was going to fit the bill nicely as the credits began to roll over a posh penthouse apartment overlooking what was obviously New York City, the accompanying music bouncy and jazzy, like something from a 1960s sex farce. The title, *Down On Love,* then came up, making Lanie frown. She hadn't seen the film when it was in theaters, but she was pretty sure it was called *Down With Love.* Oh, well. Whatever.

Within five minutes, though, Lanie could tell that this movie wasn't the same one that had played in theaters. Well, not the kind of theater she visited, anyway. Because from what she could gather, the main male character was named Donovan Love, and there was definitely someone going down on—

"Oh, my," she said when she realized that she had erroneously chosen a movie from the adult menu instead of the regular menu. "Omigosh," she elaborated when that became even more obvious with the appearance of two more scantily clad women on-screen.

"Uh, Lanie?" she heard Miles say beside her. "Are you sure this was the movie you wanted to see?"

She was shaking her head before he even finished the question, but was too frozen with mortification to switch the damned thing off. Okay, and maybe she was just a little fascinated, too, by what was happening on the screen, since she'd never in her life seen such a thing. Just exactly how did the blonde manage that position? she wondered, tilting her head to the side in an effort to study the geometry involved. And the redhead must be a gymnast to be able to do that. And the brunette was definitely double-jointed.

"Lanie?" she heard Miles's voice again. And just as it had down in the garage, it sounded like it was coming through something thick and hazy.

"Yeah?" she said, still distracted by the antics—or something—on the screen.

"I really don't think this is the movie you wanted to order. Is it?"

Finally it hit Lanie just what she was watching, with Miles sitting right there watching it with her.

"Omigosh," she muttered, pointing the remote at the TV again, this time switching it off. Then, just for good measure, she stood and threw the remote across the room, happy to see it land behind a chair where it would be difficult to retrieve. "I am so sorry," she said, feeling her face flame with embarrassment. "I just— I didn't realize— I mean, I couldn't believe— Well, it's just that I've never seen one of those— Oh, damn." And then she dropped her head into her hands and willed herself to disappear.

It didn't help that Miles started laughing. "You've never seen one of those?" he echoed. "Do you mean one of those kinds of movies or the guy's—"

"You know exactly what I mean," she said. "Of course I've seen a man's—" She growled under her breath. "I've never seen one of those movies before," she corrected herself. She dropped her hands from her face and glared at him as he now stood in front of her. "But you, I suppose, are a connoisseur."

"Not a connoisseur," he said. "But, yeah, I've seen a few."

She glared at him some more.

"Bachelor parties," he said, as if that explained it.

"Mmm," she said noncommittally.

"But the movies are never as good as the real thing."

"Well, I should hope not."

Lanie wasn't sure what made her ask the question she did after that. Whether it was having seen what was going on on the television screen, or if it was just looking at Miles and seeing him look back at her the way he was then. As if he wanted to be doing what they'd been doing on the television screen, too. Except with one woman, instead of three. She only knew that it was a question she'd wanted to ask him for a long time, and suddenly, for some reason, the time was right.

"Miles, will you kiss me?"

He smiled when she said it, but it was a knowing smile, as if he understood what she was really asking him and had just been waiting for her to put voice to the question before doing what he wanted to do, too.

Nevertheless, he replied with a question of his own. "Is that all you want me to do?"

Knowing she had to be honest with him, Lanie shook her head. But she said nothing more, not sure she trusted her voice. Or maybe it was just that she didn't trust herself. She knew Miles understood. And she did trust him.

Without hesitation, he wound his arms around her waist and pressed his mouth to hers, threading his fingers gently through the hair at her temple. As he touched her, so tentatively, so tenderly, Lanie's thoughts and feelings became a blur of unfocused sensation, making her forget all the misgivings and worries and concerns of the past few weeks. Even the events at the party this evening drifted to the back of her mind. Instinctively, she circled his lean waist with one arm, opening her fingers over the small of his back, cupping her other hand over his nape. Vaguely, she registered the warmth of his skin beneath her fingertips, the clean, fresh scent of him and the murmur of his breath mirroring her own. He sounded needy and urgent and hungry, and less instinctively and more deliberately this time, she opened her mouth beneath his.

His tongue filled her then and he tasted her thoroughly, plunging deeper inside with each new foray. Lanie felt her body going limp under the sensuous onslaught. She fisted his shirt in her fingers, gripping him at his waist, clinging to him as if letting go would mean ending her life entirely. He tightened his arm around her waist and pulled her closer, crowding his body even more fiercely against hers. Over and over he kissed her, slanting his mouth over hers, curving his palm over the crown of her head, bending her back as he tasted her more deeply still. And all she could do was continue to cling to him, because as much as he was giving her, it wasn't nearly enough.

Lanie knew what was going to happen, and she knew there was still time to halt it if she changed her mind. The other times when she had kissed Miles, she had thought herself unprepared to make love with him, but tonight, for some reason, she felt differently. Tonight she wanted to make love with him. More than wanted. She needed to make love with him. There was an urgency to her feelings for and her response to him that hadn't been there before, something determined and rapacious and demanding. Maybe it was a result of the overwhelming emotions of the evening, the sense of danger that a killer had walked among them, that a woman had been murdered in the house where they had gone for a joyful celebration. Maybe it was an innate, primal response to death that commanded a regeneration of life in return—or at least the act that was known to create life.

Or maybe it was something even more basic. Maybe Lanie just wanted Miles in the way a woman wants a man for whom she's developed…feelings. Strong feelings. Maybe she just wanted him to know that she…felt for him. And maybe she was hoping to discover that he felt for her, too.

Or maybe she just wanted Miles, period, she admitted. Wanted him in a way that she'd never wanted anything or anyone before. They'd shared heightened emotions tonight, and now they were alone to respond to them. They were out of danger now. She was safe tonight, in Miles's arms. Tonight they could be together. And in the morning…

Well, Lanie didn't want to think about the morning right now. She only wanted to think about tonight. And tonight…

Tonight was going to be amazing, she decided.

As she continued to kiss him, she moved her hands to the front of his shirt, settling a palm on each side of the row of buttons. Through the thin fabric of his shirt, she discerned the strength and heat and hardness of him, and as she pushed her hands down his torso and then pulled them back up again, she savored every ridge of solid musculature she encountered. Sensing the power and utter maleness of him through his clothing, she knew that she wanted—needed—even more.

Without hesitation, she lifted one hand to the uppermost button and freed it, pulling back enough to brave a glance at Miles's face. His hair was messier than it had been before, made so by Lanie's own hand. His cheeks were ruddy with his desire, his mouth parted in a way that made him look even hungrier than she felt herself. Silently he nodded, and she moved her hand to the next button, undoing it, too.

As she moved down the length of his shirt, unfastening each button one by one, she felt his hands on her back, moving in lazy circles, starting at her shoulders and slowly descending. His fingers connected with the zipper of her dress, which he gripped easily and tugged down. By the time she reached the waistband of his trousers and began to pull his shirttail free to finish the job, he was parting the fabric of her dress and skimming his hands over her naked back, creating a delicious friction that wound through her lower body.

Once his shirt was completely unbuttoned, she dipped her hands beneath the garment to skim it over his shoulders. She hesitated when her fingers came into contact with his unclothed body, marveling at the contradictions of him. He was hard and solid and unyielding, yet smooth and ductile and silky. Not even realizing she had intended to do it, Lanie buried her fingers in the dark hair that spanned his chest from shoulder to shoulder, loving the springy feel of him beneath her fingertips. She thumbed his flat nipples, skimmed her fingers over his rugged torso, slipped her middle finger into the divot at the base of his strong throat. His physique was just so intriguing, so different from her own, yet so wholly complementary. She just couldn't seem to touch him enough.

Even though this wasn't the first time Lanie had touched a man in passion, somehow she felt different exploring Miles. Over and over, around and about, she let her hands seek and find and investigate, until she finally did push his shirt over his shoulders, letting it cascade to the floor in a silent heap.

And then he stood before her half-naked, his expression reflecting his response to all the touching she had been doing. Every last trace of passion and wantonness and need that must be coursing through him was apparent on his face. She gasped as he yanked her against him again, and her pulse leapt wildly as he pushed her dress from her shoulders and down around her waist and began to explore her in return. Starting at her shoulders, he slowly moved his hands lower, skimming his palms over her shoulder blades, tracing her spine with his fingers, lingering at the small of her back, where he spread his hands open wide.

He dipped his head to hers again, capturing her mouth with his once more, but teasing her with the tip of his tongue this time. Leisurely, he guided it along her upper lip, and slowly…oh, so slowly…he traced it along the plump curve of her lower one. Then, nuzzling his mouth more persistently against hers, he slipped his hands low again, into the gaping fabric of her dress, over the round curve of her bottom. Lanie gasped again at the possessiveness in the gesture, and he took advantage of her response by thrusting his tongue into her mouth again, and pulling her body forward to rub her pelvis against his.

Fire shot through her at the contact, igniting in her womb and blazing outward, searing, sizzling, scalding her. Instead of retreating, however, Lanie only pushed herself more enthusiastically against him, oblivious to the fact that they were already as close as two people could be. Miles didn't seem to mind, though, only jerked at the skirt of Lanie's dress until he'd hiked it up to her waist, then closed his fingers more intimately over her derriere. His palms warmed her tender flesh through the thin fabric of her panties, but that heat doubled and then tripled when he moved his hand over the fabric, dragging it over her sensitive skin. Then he was dipping his hand under the lace of her panties, kneading her naked flesh, generating a delicious sort of friction that nearly scorched her, inside and out.

She tore her mouth from his in an effort to gasp for breath, but he immediately reclaimed it, kissing her even more deeply than before. She felt him ripen against her belly, growing long and hard, and told herself she must only be imagining the size and power of him pulsing against her. He was so...

Oh.

He must have sensed what she was thinking, and obviously wanting to confirm her suspicions, he gripped her wrist in relentless fingers and pushed her hand between their bodies, pressing her palm boldly against that part of himself. Lanie knew then that he was every bit as powerful as she had sensed, and then some. Greedily she closed her fingers over him as well as she could through the fabric of his trousers, and he groaned his approval of the gesture. He kissed her again as he folded his hand over the back of hers and pushed hard, rubbing both their fingers along the length of his hard shaft. Then back up. Then down. Over and over and over again.

As he guided her hand over himself, Miles took care to see to her needs, too, moving the hand on her bottom in time with the other. He dipped one long finger into the elegant cleft bisecting her buttocks, caressing her gently, up and down…up and down…up and down….

Never in her life had Lanie felt the way she felt in that moment, with Miles touching both himself and her with such intimate, unashamed strokes. Her entire body began to move in response, undulating against his with each new caress. At some point, though, she realized she alone was touching him, because he had moved both hands behind her, had pulled down her panties to completely bare her to the cool night air. So she moved her hands to the waistband of his trousers, thinking it might be a good idea to pull down his pants, too.

But she fumbled with his zipper when he began palming and petting the soft globes of her bottom, creasing the sensitive cleft with sure fingers. He gave one buttock a not entirely gentle squeeze as he drove one finger inside her for a soft, scant penetration, making Lanie cry out at the shocking nature of the action. Even more shocking, though, was her realization that she enjoyed the scandalous sensations that shot through her in response.

Miles must have interpreted her cry as reluctance, because he didn't repeat the action. Instead, he moved his hands to the dress bunched at her waist, pushing both it and her panties down the length of her legs, to her ankles, so that Lanie could kick off both. Then he moved his hands to her front, tracing the circle of her navel with his thumb, tripping his fingertips over her ribs, one by one, finally coming to a halt as he curved his fingers beneath the lower swell of each breast.

Reaching behind herself, Lanie freed the hooks of her brassiere, loosening the garment enough that Miles could push his hands up beneath the lacy fabric and over her naked skin. Gently, he kneaded her flesh before capturing an erect little bud, rolling it tenderly between his fingers and flicking his thumb against it. And then he was pushing her breast higher and bending his head lower, sucking as much of her into his mouth as he could. He first laved her with the flat of his tongue, then taunted her with its tip, and then he simply savored her, over and over again. As he held her firm in one hand and continued to taste her with his mouth, he dropped his other hand low again, reaching between her thighs and skimming his fingers along the sensitive flesh there.

Lanie gripped his shoulders hard in her hands, feeling as if she might just melt away under his tender ministrations. Just when she was certain she would indeed dissolve into a languid puff of steam, he upped the ante again, moving his fingers higher, slipping them between her legs to that most sensitive, clandestine part of her.

Oh, she thought then. Oh, my.

Oh…Miles!

She gasped as he penetrated her deeply with one long finger and then slowly withdrew it. Immediately he repeated the action, going even deeper this time, pairing it with a few caresses at her threshold that left her thrashing with need. The way he touched her after that was positively sinful. So erotic. Hypnotic. Narcotic.

And still not nearly enough.

"Miles," she gasped. "Oh, Miles. Oh, please."

Whether she was begging him to slow down or speed up, Lanie honestly couldn't have said. Part of her wanted him to go slower, so that she might think about what was happening, weigh the consequences and be sure it was what she wanted. But another part of her wanted him to go faster, until she didn't have time for doubts or concerns.

He must have thought she was asking for the latter, because he slid a second finger inside her, spreading them, opening her, moving them in and out with a steady rhythm that matched the beating of her heart. Deeper and deeper he penetrated her with each foray, until she fancied she could feel him nearly touching her heart. A third finger joined the two, filling her completely then, but somehow she still didn't quite feel full enough.

"Miles," she tried again, his name barely a gasp this time. "Please. Please, you have to—"

"What?" he interrupted her, the single word hot and damp against her naked breast. He traced her nipple with the tip of his tongue, eliciting another frantic, incoherent cry from deep inside her.

"Please," she managed to say. But he drove his fingers against and inside her again, and she found it impossible to say more.

Evidently that one word was enough, though, because Miles straightened and lifted her into his arms, then carried her into the bedroom and set her in the center of the already turned-down bed. Lanie watched intently, shamelessly, as he shed his trousers and boxer shorts. And she realized she hadn't been mistaken at all about the size and power of him. He was magnificent in his nudity, clearly confident of both his appearance and his prowess. He looked like a man who knew what he wanted, and who knew exactly what to do and say to get it. He looked eager to please, as well, and she was certain he knew exactly what to say and do to achieve that, too.

Smiling, she extended her hand to him in silent invitation, and Miles joined her on the bed without hesitation, lying on his side next to her. He pulled her close and kissed her again, tracing a finger down along the curves and valleys of her naked side—from her jaw, to her shoulder, to her breast, then to the dip and swell of her waist and hip, and lower still, to her thigh. Then he retraced the same route backward. Finally, though, he took her hand in his and rolled onto his back, tugging her atop him. Lanie straddled his lean, hard torso, closing her bent knees against him, tangling her fingers in the dark hair on his chest. He grinned as he filled both hands with her breasts, thumbing the sensitive peaks, tracing the ample circles of her areolae.

"You are so beautiful," he murmured.

The remark didn't seem to require a response. Not a verbal one, at any rate. So Lanie splayed her hands over the warm skin of his chest, gently fingered the ridges and bumps of his flawless musculature, telling him without words that she thought he was beautiful, too.

He caressed her breasts for a few moments more, then skimmed his hands down over her flat stomach to settle them on the curve of each hip. Gently, he pulled her forward, creating a slow, insistent friction between her legs that was quite extraordinary. When he heard her soft moan of satisfaction, he pushed her backward again—a bit less gently this time, and the friction was a bit wilder—leaving a damp trail on his flesh in her wake. Again and again, she rode his strong body up and down, until Miles finally halted her by moving her completely forward and lifting her hips from his chest. He moved his own body down a little as he did, and for a moment, Lanie wasn't sure what he was trying to do. Then she felt his mouth open against the slick center of her, and all she could do was grasp the headboard and hang on.

No shy little taste or tentative sampling first. No, Miles went right to devouring her. She felt the flat of his tongue lap up and down against her, and glanced down to see him with his eyes closed, feasting upon her as if she were the most delectable treat he'd ever encountered. He gripped her bottom firmly in both hands and held her in place as he consumed her, his hunger fierce, his appetite slow to be satisfied. Eventually, though, he gentled his actions, tapping at her tiny bud with the tip of his tongue, dipping it between each delicate fold of flesh, then penetrating her as deeply as he could.

Never in her life had any man paid such care to that part of her, and Lanie didn't think she would ever be satisfied with another man again. Miles's oral attentions seemed to go on forever, until tiny white-hot explosions of pleasure began to ripple through her. Her orgasm was long and thorough, but instead of satisfying her, it only made her hungry for more. Miles seemed to understand immediately, because he pushed her body back down along his torso until she felt his long, hard member pressing against her fanny. Needing him inside her, she pushed herself up on her knees to rise above him. Then Miles urged her body down over his, until he began to part her with his thick, heavy staff.

"I like it fast and hard the first time," he said. "Is that okay with you?"

The first time, Lanie repeated to herself. Meaning he fully intended for there to be more than one coupling tonight. She found his confidence and conviction utterly arousing, as was the promise of a long night of thorough lovemaking. She nodded her reply and braced herself for his penetration. It was swift, deep and complete. And never in her life had Lanie felt fuller or more satisfied than she did in that moment.

He filled her completely, entirely, until she was convinced the two of them had melded into one. He bucked his body upward, taking her with him for the ride, going still deeper inside her. Again and again, he jerked his hips up against hers, his long, hard shaft going deeper each time, making Lanie wonder if he might split her in two. Then he pulled her down against him and rolled their bodies on the bed, withdrawing from her until he was behind her, his front pressed to her back, and he entered her from behind.

She liked this way even better, she decided, when he moved his hand over her waist and down between her legs, fondling her as he penetrated her. His other hand massaged her breast, until Lanie wasn't sure she could tolerate the myriad sensations winding through her body. For long moments he continued to take her that way, then he turned their bodies again, so that she was on her back facing him. He rose up on his knees between her legs and circled her ankles with sure fingers, then spread her legs wide and vaulted himself inside her again. Lanie gripped the sides of the pillow with both hands and held on for all she could, crying out as Miles increased his already rapid rhythm.

Heat began to build inside her then, moving outward in concentric circles with each new thrust of his body into hers. Just as those circles exploded into a white-hot arc of pleasure, she heard him cry out his own release, felt him spill hotly inside her.

He collapsed against her, and just like that, as quickly as the storm had come, it began to recede. Carefully, Miles rolled to his side, bringing Lanie with him, their bodies still joined together. He held her close, twining a distracted hand into her hair. He kissed her temple with unbelievable tenderness, and somehow, it brought her even closer to him than their frantic coupling had. Then he gazed down into her eyes. He said nothing, but at the same time, he seemed to be telling her everything she wanted to hear.

Lanie, heaven help her, had no idea how to respond. So she only moved her hand to his face and cupped his cheek, then lifted her head enough to press her mouth gently against his. Then, nearly overcome with exhaustion—both physical and emotional—she lay her head down on his chest and closed her eyes. The last thing she remembered before sleep claimed her was the sound of Miles speaking her name. She wasn't sure, but she thought he may have said something else, too, something she tried very hard to understand, but that somehow just didn't seem real....

Eleven

Lanie awoke slowly, feeling groggy and disoriented, as if she'd had too much to drink the night before. But that wasn't possible, because she'd been too busy dancing with Miles to finish even one drink, let alone too many. Gradually, though, she remembered what had happened, how the two of them had turned to each other time and time again during the night, and she smiled. Okay, so it wasn't that she'd had too much to drink last night. It was that she'd had too much Miles.

Immediately, though, she knew that wasn't true, either. There was no such thing as too much Miles.

Her eyes still closed, she nestled more deeply into the covers, reveling in the feel of him still sleeping behind her. His naked body was pressed against hers, his front to her back, her head tucked under his chin, his leg draped over her thigh. One arm was roped over her waist, his hand loosely cradling her breast. She smiled when she realized he was fully erect, pushing against her fanny in a way that made heat wind through her again. Reaching behind herself, Lanie took him in her hand and caressed him, loving the way he grew even fuller in her palm as she touched him. He groaned sleepily in response, but she knew he was awake when he shifted his body to better facilitate her actions. The hand below her breast moved higher, covering the rounded flesh completely for a moment before dipping low, between her legs.

She was already damp there, and he furrowed his fingers easily through the sensitive folds. As he touched her, he slid into her from behind, moving slow and deep and very nearly taking her breath away. Again and again he entered her, bringing her awake in a way she could very easily grow accustomed to experiencing every morning.

For long moments, they coupled that way, languidly, passionately, until the little ripples of delight began to wind through her again. He quickened his pace, plunging in more forcefully, and Lanie pushed her body backward in response. With one final, incandescent thrust, Miles exploded inside her, and Lanie cried out in answering delight.

She loved this man to whom she was engaged, she realized then. More than she had ever loved anyone before. If only the engagement were real, she thought. If only he loved her, too.

"I could easily get used to waking up like that every morning," Miles murmured against her damp hair. "Oh, God, Lanie, the things you make me feel."

Was one of those things love? she wondered. But even before the question was fully formed in her brain, she knew the answer to it. Miles didn't love her. He wasn't the sort of man to fall in love. Oh, certainly he liked her. Maybe he even felt affection for her. No man could make love to a woman the way he had made love to her last night without there being some measure of honest emotion involved. But it wasn't love, she knew. Not on his part, anyway.

But that was okay, she told herself. She felt enough love for two people this morning. Somehow, though, the realization of that didn't exactly make her feel happy.

She schooled her features into as contented an expression as she could as she rolled over and wrapped her arms around Miles's neck. Crowding herself against him, she covered his mouth with hers and kissed him for all she was worth. He pulled her close and rolled onto his back, bringing her along with him, so that she was half lying atop him by the time they ended the kiss. He let his hands wander freely over her bare back and bottom as he held her, and Lanie decided then that there was a very good chance she would never leave the bed again.

"Last night was amazing," Miles told her with a smile.

She smiled back, this one feeling almost genuine. "It was that," she agreed.

"I don't think I've ever made love that many times in one sitting," he said.

"Well, we were only sitting one time," she reminded him. "All those others—"

He halted her with a quick kiss. "Don't start talking about it," he cautioned her. "Or else you'll get me all turned on again."

Lanie moved against his lower half, where he still stood at half-mast. "I'm beginning to think you never turn off."

He gave her bottom an affectionate squeeze. "Not when you're in the same room I don't," he told her.

She captured a strand of dark hair that had fallen over his forehead and wound it around her finger. "I don't think I ever want to leave this bed again," she said, speaking aloud her thoughts of a moment ago.

"Fine with me," he told her. "We can order room service again. And again. And again."

"We keep doing that, the hotel staff is going to start thinking we're on our honeymoon."

"Nah," Miles said. "Everyone knows we're getting married on Valentine's Day. It's been in all the papers. They'll just think we're getting in a lot of practice between now and then."

His mention of the wedding made Lanie remember something very important, and her gaze flew to the clock on the nightstand. She relaxed immediately, though, when she realized it was still early and that they had plenty of time.

"I hate to remind you of this," she said, "especially since I just told you I don't ever want to leave this bed, but... We're meeting my parents for lunch today. And then we're supposed to go to that big bridal expo with my mom."

Miles closed his eyes and groaned at the reminder. "Damn. I forgot all about it."

"Me, too. And I'd say we could skip it," she offered, "but Dad arranged to have some media people there so it could be a photo op for us. I'm sure he'll finagle a way to tag along."

Miles blew out an exasperated sound. "You know, somebody ought to tell him he can stop campaigning, now that he's won the election."

She smiled halfheartedly. "I'll put it on my to-do list. I'm sorry, Miles."

Miles looked at Lanie, thinking she sounded genuinely

apologetic. But whether she was sorry specifically because they had to go to a wedding show, or sorry for the simple reason that they'd have to eventually get dressed and leave their bed, Miles couldn't have said. He hoped it was the latter. Because he was sorry, too. Not about the wedding show, which could potentially be kind of fun—provided he was there with Lanie, naturally—but for the simple reason that it felt so good lying here naked with her, talking, sharing, planning the day ahead.

Funny, he thought then, but he was almost enjoying the morning after more than he'd enjoyed the night before. And that *really* wasn't like him. Normally, he couldn't get out of bed fast enough the morning after making love to a woman. Many times, he didn't even stay long enough for there to even *be* a morning after. And when there was, he didn't usually waste it talking. With Lanie, though, talking didn't feel like a waste at all. Talking felt perfectly normal. Perfectly natural. Perfectly right.

Hell, it just felt perfect. And that, too, was something Miles had never experienced with a woman before.

"I don't know why Mom is so insistent that we keep up this charade now that Dad's won the election," Lanie continued, oblivious to Miles's train of thought. "It's really not necessary at this point."

He shrugged it off quite literally. "I don't mind," he told her. And he was surprised to realize he truly didn't. "For one thing, people do still seem to be watching us pretty closely. I don't know if you noticed last night, but there were a lot of people at the party who seemed to take more than a passing interest in what we were doing."

"I did notice, actually," she told him. "It kind of ticked me off."

He smiled. Strangely, Miles hadn't minded so much. "And for another thing," he added, "it could actually be kind of fun, going to this expo thing. I've never been to a wedding show before. What are they like?"

"I have no idea," she said. "I've never been to one, either." She snuggled closer to him in the bed. "From what I gather, it's a bunch of vendors who sell or arrange wedding stuff all organized conveniently under one roof. Florists, photographers, caterers, that kind of thing. I mean, what else would there be?"

Miles gave that some thought. Just what did people do for weddings these days? he wondered. He was surprised to find that he was honestly curious about such a thing. "Hmm," he said. "Musicians maybe, for the reception."

"Some people use DJs," Lanie said.

Miles shook his head. "Nah. I'd want a live band for my reception."

He felt her nod beside him, her hair falling over his naked chest, feeling pleasant in a completely asexual way that he'd never imagined a woman could make him feel. "I think a live band would be preferable, too," she agreed. "Jazz, though, not country and western."

Miles feigned shock. "You don't like country music? A nice Texas girl like you?"

"I like it okay," she said. "But I like jazz better."

He smiled. "Okay. We can have a jazz band. But they better know a few country standards."

"Fine," she said, smiling back. "I could go along with that."

"And it would have to be a church wedding," he said. "None of this justice of the peace stuff."

Now she turned to look up at him. "I thought we were

going to get married at the governor's mansion," Lanie said. "That's what my father told the reporters."

"That was just a red herring," Miles said decisively. "Something to throw the media off our trail, since you and I want a small, intimate affair with only family and close friends. We're really going to have the ceremony at church."

"Mmm," Lanie murmured. "Of course, your family being what it is, that sort of negates that whole *small* concept."

"Good point."

"So maybe a church wedding really would be better," she agreed.

Miles grinned again and turned onto one side, propping his hand against his head to study Lanie head-on. This was kind of fun, planning a phony wedding. They could have whatever they wanted, cost and convenience be damned.

"What colors?" he asked.

She narrowed her eyes at him. "What do you mean, what colors?"

"What's the color scheme for the wedding going to be?"

Now Lanie grinned, too, obviously having fun with the whole faux nuptials, just as he was. "Pink," she told him, chuckling when he grimaced in response.

"Pink?" he exclaimed.

"Pink," she insisted. "Baby-pink. Petal-pink. The softest pink you can imagine."

Miles made a face. "What about navy blue?" he asked.

"Pink," Lanie told him.

"Dark green?" he asked hopefully.

"Pink," she said.

"Harvest gold?"

"Pink."

"Bloodred?"

"Pink."

"Turquoise."

"Piiiiiiiiiink."

He sighed. "Fine. Pink."

"Petal-pink," she corrected him.

"Petal-pink," he agreed, doing his best not to gag.

"And the groomsmen can wear gray," she said. "Morning coats and ascots."

"Oh, no," Miles told her. "I get to pick what the groomsmen wear. And it's going to be black. Traditional black tuxedos. With bow ties."

"But I want an afternoon wedding," she said, grinning in a way that told him she was only saying it to needle him. "Morning coats would be better."

"Evening wedding," he told her. "After dark."

"Vocalist," she decided. "A vocalist who'll sing 'Wind Beneath My Wings' just before we take our vows."

"Oh, I don't think so," he countered. "We can do the vocalist, but she'll sing 'Free Bird.'"

Lanie stuck her tongue out at that. "'Love Will Keep Us Together,'" she suggested instead.

"Maybe we should just stick with an organist," Miles replied.

"Fine," she conceded with clear reluctance. "But that means we get to have white cake at the reception."

"Chocolate," he corrected her.

"Hazelnut."

"Chocolate."

"Amaretto."

"Chocolate."

She frowned at him. "Champagne fountain."

He shook his head. "Open bar."

She expelled an exasperated sound. "Boy, good thing we're going to a wedding show," she said. "We need a lot of help with this thing."

"No, we don't," he told her. "It's going to be a formal evening ceremony at church, with a live band at the reception, no vocalist, chocolate cake and open bar."

"No," she said, "it's going to be a semiformal afternoon ceremony at church, with a live band at the reception, no vocalist, white cake and champagne fountain."

"You got it partly right," he said with a grin.

She made that impatient sound again. "Oh, why can't you just be like other grooms and not give a damn about the wedding preparations?"

"Hey, it's my wedding, too!" he reminded her. "You only get married once, you know. I want the day to be special as much as you do."

Lanie opened her mouth to say something in response to that, then closed it again without speaking. But her gaze never left his, and he could tell by her expression that she was thinking about something she really wanted to say, but for some reason couldn't.

"What?" he asked. "What is it?"

"Nothing," she replied quickly.

A little too quickly, Miles thought. "C'mon," he cajoled. "You were going to say something. What is it?"

She eyed him intently for another minute, then said, "Just that…if someone didn't know better, they'd think we were really planning a wedding here."

"If *someone* didn't know better?" he echoed slowly, cautiously. With only a small hesitation, he then added, "Or if *we* didn't know better?"

Lanie's eyes went wide at that. "Do we know better?" she asked in the same quiet, careful tone of voice Miles had been using.

"I don't know," he told her, still trying to read her mind, still frustrated at not being able to. "Do we?"

She shook her head slowly, but she seemed to be studying him the same way, as if she were making every effort to get a handle on his thoughts. Finally, though, she said, "I don't know, either."

"I think you do," he said experimentally.

"And I think you do, too," she immediately replied.

"Lanie—"

"Miles—"

They spoke as one and halted as one, neither seeming willing then to say whatever they had intended to say.

"I really wish I knew what you were thinking right now," he finally admitted.

"Why?" she asked.

"Because I want to know if it's the same thing I'm thinking."

"Then tell me what you're thinking, and I'll let you know if it's the same thing I'm thinking."

Yeah, he'd been thinking that was what she was going to say. In spite of that, Miles took his time forming his reply. Mostly because he couldn't quite believe he was thinking what he'd been thinking for the past several minutes—ever since he and Lanie had started planning their phony wedding. Like how, at some point, the wedding he was planning didn't really feel phony. It felt real. He'd honestly started picturing in his mind's eye what it would be like to walk down the aisle with Lanie Meyers. That could only be because he'd been thinking, whether consciously or not, what it would be like to be married to Lanie Meyers. As in, after the wedding. As in white picket fences and rug rats and Sunday barbecues. As in happily ever after.

As in forever.

Was that possible? Miles asked himself now. And if so, when had it happened? He'd never once entertained, even in passing, a fantasy about being married to anyone. Oh, sure, whenever he'd heard a friend was getting married, he'd start wondering about the whole marriage thing and whether it was for him. But never in terms of joining himself to one woman in particular. When Miles had considered the whole marriage thing, it had been in vague terms of what if…?

Ultimately, he'd always found himself dwelling on the negatives, never giving much thought to the positives—mostly because he'd figured there couldn't be too many positives in a marriage. His freedom would be limited, maybe even nonexistent. He'd have obligations toward and responsibilities for someone other than himself. He'd have to keep another person apprised of his comings and goings all the time. He couldn't just take off on the spur of the moment and do whatever he wanted whenever he wanted to do it. He'd always have to take someone else's feelings into consideration. He'd be tied down to one person for the rest of his life. Yada yada yada.

But what if that person was Lanie?

He gave that some thought now, too. Would it be so awful, being tied down to her? Being obliged to and responsible for her? There hadn't been a single moment over the last few weeks when he'd felt as if his freedom was inhibited. On the contrary, she'd been like a breath of fresh air. Keeping her apprised of his comings and goings hadn't felt like imprisonment at all. It had made him feel good, knowing that he cared enough about her to let her know where he was, and he appreciated the fact that she cared about him enough to want to know. They'd done lots of things on the spur of the moment, and it had been even more fun being spontaneous with another person. And taking her feelings into consideration along with his own had felt totally natural to Miles, almost as if their feelings were one and the same.

When had that happened? he asked himself again. When had he started thinking in terms of himself and Lanie, instead of just himself?

He tried to remember. But he couldn't. From the moment he and Lanie had started talking that night at the fund-raiser, he'd felt completely comfortable, as if he'd known her forever, as if she were a part of him. Maybe the reason he'd capitulated without much of a fight to her father's demand that they pretend to be engaged was due to that as much as anything else.

Or maybe it was because, even then, Miles had known he was falling in love with her.

Wow. Love. He'd never imagined he could fall in love like that with anyone. To the point where he started making subconscious plans to spend the rest of his life with her. But he realized now that that was what he had been doing for the past three weeks with this allegedly phony engagement. Somewhere in the back of his brain, at some point in the game, to Miles it had stopped being phony.

"Marry me, Lanie," he said suddenly, impulsively.

But the minute the words were out of his mouth, he knew they weren't sudden or impulsive at all. Proposing to Lanie felt like the most natural, most wonderful thing in the world. He couldn't imagine why he hadn't done it before now.

Her eyes went wide at his declaration. "What?"

He smiled. "Marry me," he said again. "For real, I mean. You're right, anyone listening in on our conversation just now would have thought we were planning a real, honest-to-God wedding. And that could only be because, on some level, we both want it to be real and honest-to-God."

"Miles, I—" A funny little hiccup of sound escaped her, and she smiled. "Are you serious?"

"Of course I'm serious," he told her. "I think we should get married."

"But…why?"

He thought it was the stupidest question he'd ever heard in his life—until he remembered that neither he nor Lanie had said a word about the reason people traditionally decided to get married.

And, no, it wasn't for the tax break.

In spite of his conviction, though, Miles suddenly had trouble putting voice to the words. Probably, he thought, because he'd never said them to anyone before.

So he sidestepped it by saying, "Isn't it obvious?"

She narrowed her eyes at him in a way he immediately decided he didn't like. "Not really," she told him.

"Last night didn't tell you everything you need to know?" he asked.

"Last night told me that you and I are incredible together," she said.

"Exactly," he told her, smiling.

But his smile fell when she qualified, "Sexually speaking."

"But what about emotionally?" he asked.

"What about it?"

This time, Miles was the one to emit an exasperated sound. They were going to tap-dance around it all day if one of them didn't just come right out and say it. "I love you, Lanie Meyers," he told her. Certainly. Unequivocally. "And I want you to be my wife."

For a minute, she stared at him as if she couldn't quite believe he had just said what he had. And for that minute, Miles wondered if it was possible that he was the only one whose heart was involved. Maybe Lanie didn't love him, too, he thought. The idea honestly hadn't occurred to him until now. She'd seemed to enjoy their time together over the past few weeks as much as he had, and she'd responded to him last night with equal passion and equal hunger. He'd just assumed she must feel the same way about him as he felt about her. He'd just assumed that if he was in love, Lanie must be, too.

But what if she wasn't?

Never in his life had Miles experienced the terror that shot through him in that moment. What if Lanie said no? What if she didn't want to marry him? How could he live the rest of his life alone? Because he realized in that moment that by falling in love with Lanie, he'd closed the door on the possibility of it happening with anyone else. Hell, he was thirty-six years old and had never felt for any woman the way he'd managed to feel for her in a matter of weeks. Days. Hours. And that could only be because there *was* no other woman for him. Lanie was it. She was The One. And now, if she didn't love him back…

He couldn't even finish the thought. Because if Lanie didn't love him…

"Yes," she said softly, bringing his troubled thoughts to a crashing halt. She smiled almost shyly. "I'll marry you."

But even after hearing her say the words, Miles still couldn't quite believe it was true. "Really?" he asked, smiling tentatively. "You'll marry me?"

"Of course I'll marry you," she said. She cupped her hand over his jaw, and her smile went supernova. "Oh, Miles. I've been in love with you since that first night at the fund-raiser. Even before I met you, I think I was half in love with you. Meeting you, talking to you, being with you... I can't imagine being with anyone else," she told him. "I just want to be with you. Always. Forever. I can't believe you want that, too. I love you so much."

"Then I think you and I ought to make this wedding for real."

She smiled. "I think you're right."

He reached for her, threading his fingers through the long silk of her hair. "Just one thing, though, sweetheart," he told her before brushing his lips lightly over hers.

"What's that?" she sighed back, circling her arm around his neck.

He grinned at her. "It's going to be chocolate cake."

She grinned back, nibbling his lower lip with her teeth. "White cake," she whispered softly.

"Chocolate."

"White."

"Choc—"

But Miles didn't get any further than that. Well, not with words, anyway.

Twelve

Lanie's first impulse was to tell her parents over lunch that she and Miles were going to be tying the knot for real. But her father wasn't in the greatest of moods, she saw when they arrived at the restaurant, and her mother looked exhausted, so Lanie figured maybe it would be better to wait. She'd all but forgotten the tragedy of the previous evening during the revels and revelations of the morning. Her parents, however, understandably hadn't been able to put it out of their minds. Although news of an engagement—a real one this time— would have certainly lifted their spirits, something made Lanie hesitate. The timing just didn't feel right.

Ultimately, over the course of lunch, all four of them decided that perhaps, all things considered, today might not be a good time for festivity and celebration. They'd all been present at a murder the night before, and attending a wedding expo the day after might give the appearance of callousness. Even after winning himself a second term in office, to Lanie's father, appearances were still important. Even so, in spite of her newly engaged status, Lanie wasn't inclined to attend such a festive event, either.

Really, she would have rather spent the day with Miles, anyway, just the two of them, alone. The feelings they had so recently acknowledged for each other were so new, and she wanted time to get used to them before sharing them with other people. She still couldn't quite believe Miles loved her, too, that he wanted to marry her. It would probably take some time for that to set in. For now she was content to just be with him, enjoying the new concept of a happily ever after with him.

As much appeal as the thought of returning to bed with him held, in the long run they decided to stay out and do fun stuff together. After lunch, they somehow ended up at a shopping mall, and then in the bridal registry of one of the department stores. Lanie told the consultant they only wanted to look, but the woman recognized them and knew they were engaged. When she discovered they weren't registered anywhere yet, she was adamant that they fill out a form that very day because people wouldn't want to wait until the last minute to start shopping for the bride and groom.

Which was how Lanie and Miles found themselves trying to figure out which china, crystal and silver patterns they both liked, deciding on the color schemes for a bathroom and bedroom and kitchen in a house neither of them owned and wondering what the hell a duvet was.

It was fun, though, Lanie had to admit. And at the end of the day, when they returned to Miles's hotel suite again, it felt totally natural to turn to each other in passion, as they had the night before. This time, though, knowing they would be spending the rest of their lives together, their lovemaking took on a dimension that hadn't been there before. Where last night there had been an almost desperate quality to their coupling, this time there was a hopeful, enthusiastic, confident sort of passion unlike anything Lanie had ever felt before.

She loved this man, she thought again, getting more used to the idea—and the emotion—now. Loved him with all her heart and soul. And he loved her, too, as deeply and with equal conviction. So much so that the two of them never wanted to be apart again. Nothing on earth could have made Lanie happier. Nothing.

Tomorrow, she told herself as she cuddled against Miles hours after they went to bed, as sleep finally, slowly, claimed her. Tomorrow she would tell her parents the news about her and Miles. And she knew they would be as ecstatic as she.

Lanie's father was working at his desk in his personal office—the one that was off-limits to the media and state employees, but always open to family members—when she arrived at the governor's mansion the following afternoon. She liked this room much better than the official governor's domain, because this one contained so many of her father's personal possessions, and it reflected the man beneath the gruff exterior. As often as she and her father had butted heads during her life, and although they didn't always see eye to eye, and although Tom Meyers could be more than a little difficult to live with during times of stress, Lanie knew that deep down he was a decent guy.

Although there were those who were convinced that politics corrupted people, she knew her father's convictions and ethics and morals had remained unchanged during all the years he had held public office. His politics might not always be in step with her own, but his reasons for feeling the way he did were good ones, and he was thoughtful and careful when forming his policies.

He was just a good guy, that was all, despite his blustering and concerns for appearances. Election years were always tougher than others, and Lanie and her mother both had learned to live with Tom Meyers during those pressure-filled times, knowing he would ease up once his position was secure. The past few months had been especially difficult, with his opponent gaining so much in the polls and her father fearing that he might not win a second term. Under normal conditions, he would have handled the photos of Lanie and Miles in the newspapers with considerably less irrationality and significantly more common sense, but...

She smiled as she strode toward where he sat with his back to her. Everything had turned out for the best, she told herself. Yes, her father had put his interests first in the matter, but Lanie knew he'd been acting on her behalf, too. He'd wanted to protect her from innuendo and bad-mouthing as much as he'd wanted to preserve his own image. He cared about her as much as he cared about himself. Had he not insisted on the phony engagement, she and Miles might never have had the chance to fall in love. What had started off as a horrible misunderstanding that might have ruined more than one life had, in the long run, made so many lives better. Lanie's and Miles's especially. For that, she would always be grateful for her father's overreaction.

"Dad?" she said as she approached him now.

"Well, hello there, young lady!" he said without looking up from his work.

He was dressed casually, she saw, in brown trousers and a wheat-colored cardigan sweater, the way he normally was on weekends, away from the public eye. And he was obviously in a much better mood today than he had been yesterday. Lanie was glad. It was a shame Ryan Fortune's big night had been marred by such a terrible event. But one good thing had come of it. She'd heard on the news that Ryan was no longer a suspect in Christopher Jamison's death and that the police were now attributing it to Jason Wilkes, who had turned out to be Christopher's brother, Jason Jamison. Lanie just hoped that now Ryan Fortune—all the Fortunes, in fact—would be able to put this regrettable episode behind them.

"What a nice surprise to have you visit today," her father continued. He glanced over his shoulder to smile briefly at her, then went back to doing whatever he was doing.

"Is Mom around?" Lanie asked.

"She had a luncheon of some kind, I believe," her father told her. "I hope that won't keep you from visiting."

Lanie smiled at his easygoing tone of voice and posture. What a difference from the man before the election who was fearful and worried and apprehensive. This was the man who was really her father. This was the man she could talk to, the man she could reason with, the man she could laugh with.

The one with whom she could share good news.

Miles had offered to come with her when she told her parents they were engaged for real now, but Lanie had discouraged him. In spite of her parents' busyness while she was growing up that had left her in the care of others, Lanie had still managed to develop a relationship with them that was unique to the only-child experience. There had been many times in her life when the three of them had felt like one unit, and on those occasions, a fourth person just wouldn't have felt quite right. Not that she didn't want to include Miles in everything that her family did from now on, but for some reason, breaking the news of her engagement—her *real* engagement—seemed like something she should do herself.

But she wanted to do it when both of her parents were present. Her mother's absence was going to delay that, unfortunately. Still, as her father had said, there was no reason why she should cut her visit short. So she brushed a hand over her emerald-green sweater and blue jeans and strode the short distance to his desk, with the intention of seating herself in one of the leather-bound chairs opposite where he himself sat.

She came to a halt, however, before making the complete circuit around his desk, because as she passed, she glanced over to see what he was working on, which, at first glance, appeared to be paying bills and balancing the checkbook. As she started to look away, though, a name recorded in the check registry jumped out at her. Now, why on earth would Miles's name be in her father's check registry? Driving her gaze to the side of the checkbook, she saw a check sitting on the desk beside her father's right hand, and, sure enough, it was made out to Miles Fortune. Lanie looked at the amount, and her eyes went wide.

A hundred thousand dollars? She gasped to herself. Why would her father be writing Miles a check for *a hundred thousand dollars?*

"Dad?" she said, barely able to manage even that small word. She swallowed with some difficulty before continuing, hoping to ease the dryness that had overtaken her mouth and throat. But her voice still sounded hoarse when she continued, "Why are you giving Miles that much money?"

"Hmm?" he said, looking up, clearly distracted by what he was doing. He studied her blankly for a minute, then smiled. "Oh, I'm just making good on a promise," he said. "The way a good governor should."

A sick feeling opened up in the pit of Lanie's stomach. "What do you mean?"

"For playing his part in the mock engagement," he told Lanie, his tone of voice indicating she should already know that. "I promised him he'd be compensated for going along with everything the way he did. I couldn't expect him to do it for nothing."

Instead of enlightening her, though, her father's comment only made her more confused. "But..." she began. Unfortunately, no other words emerged from her mouth to finish the statement. Probably because no other words formed in her brain.

"But you know, Miles wasn't the only one who made a sacrifice," her father went on, oblivious to Lanie's distress. "You put your life on hold, too," he said. "You made the same sacrifices. You should be compensated, too." He poised his pen over the checkbook and began to write. "I should give you the same amount I'm giving him," her father said decisively, obviously thinking that was fair, when really, Lanie thought, it was anything but. "I don't know why that's just now occurring to me. Election-year craziness, I guess. You can finally buy yourself that new Jag," he said, chuckling, knowing Lanie was a fan of the car.

Oh, but a new Jaguar would certainly make her feel so much better about the way things were going.

Her father signed the check with a flourish, then turned around to hand it to Lanie. "Don't spend it all in one place," he said.

But she only shook her head. "I won't be spending it at all," she told him.

Her father looked puzzled. "Why not? You've earned it."

Somehow Lanie held back the bitter laughter she felt burning in the pit of her stomach. Although she had no idea what made her say it, since it had nothing to do with what she and her father were talking about, she told him, "I came here today to tell you and Mom that Miles and I are engaged. For real, I mean. He proposed to me yesterday morning, and I said yes."

Now her father narrowed his eyes at her, looking concerned. "What did you say?"

Forgetting that she had wanted to reveal the news to both of her parents together—then again, it was dawning on Lanie that the engagement she had thought was real actually *was* a farce—she repeated, "I came here to tell you that Miles and I are engaged for real. That we're in love." At least, she had thought they were. "And we decided to really get married." Her gaze drifted between the check her father held in his hand made out to her and the one lying on his desk made out to Miles. "But now I'm beginning to wonder if any of that is true at all."

Her father studied her in silence for a minute, not looking particularly happy about the news of her engagement. But then, why should she be surprised? Lanie asked herself. Suddenly, she wasn't feeling all that happy about the news herself.

"Miles asked you to marry him?" her father said. "For real?"

Lanie nodded weakly.

Her father's snowy eyebrows knitted downward. "Well, hell, I hope he's not expecting two hundred thousand now. I was only kidding about that."

Lanie hadn't thought she could feel any worse than she already did, but her father's remark, even though she wasn't sure she understood it, managed to make her spirits plummet even further. Not wanting to know the answer but needing to hear it, she asked, "What are you talking about?"

Her father blew out an irritated sigh. "Well, when I told Miles I expected him to go along with this pretend engagement, I assured him that he'd be well compensated. I told him I'd pay him the hundred thousand dollars for his trouble and for giving up so much of his life for a few months. I figured it was fair enough. Figured it was the right thing to do."

For his trouble, Lanie repeated to herself miserably. Because what else would it be to be engaged to her, except troubling? Naturally, it would only be fair and right to pay Miles for having to endure such a thing.

"And then," her father continued, oblivious to her distress, "I kind of jokingly told him that hell, if he'd marry you for real, I'd double the amount. But I thought he realized I was only kidding. I'd never stoop to such a thing. Besides, I knew neither one of you would want to get married."

No way they'd want to get married, Lanie repeated that to herself, too. Of course not. Not Miles, anyway. He wouldn't want to marry her—or anyone—for real. Not unless there was a two-hundred-thousand-dollar check waiting for him after the ceremony. Oh, God...

Oh, Miles...

She couldn't believe he would do that, couldn't believe he would betray her in such a way. What kind of man offered to marry a woman in exchange for money? Lanie almost laughed aloud at herself for asking the question. Who was she kidding? There were a lot of men out there who would marry a woman in exchange for money. Especially six figures. Hell, men had murdered women for a lot less than that. Why not marry one? Then you could have the added benefit of sex whenever you wanted it, too.

She still couldn't believe it. All this time Miles had only been pretending to love her? For money? Here she'd been thinking he'd agreed to go along with the charade because he was an honorable man who cared about her. She'd thought he had fallen in love with her the way she'd fallen in love with him. But he'd only agreed to do it for money. Was any part of what they'd shared real? At this point she honestly couldn't have said.

Nor could she have said what she was feeling right now. She was too confused to be able to make sense of any of it. In less than a month, Lanie had gone from having an adolescent-type crush on a man she'd never met before, to having a tenuous agreement with him, to getting to know and like him, to falling in love with him, to making love with him in a way she'd never made love before, to agreeing to spend the rest of her life with him, to finding out the only reason he'd wanted any of those things was to put a pile of money in his pocket.

In short, she felt as if she'd been hit with a brick. And until she figured it out, she didn't want to see Miles. She didn't want to see anyone. Without another word to her father and fighting back the tears, Lanie bolted from his office, heedless to his cries of "Lanie!" that followed her. She wanted out of there. Wanted to be away from everything that reminded her of her father, his political campaign and the farce that was her life.

But more than that, she wanted to be far away from Miles. And she wasn't sure she ever wanted to see him again.

When Miles answered the knock at the door to his hotel suite barely an hour after Lanie had left, he figured it would be her returning because she hadn't caught up with her parents. He was glad he'd gone ahead and showered and changed into a pair of reasonably decent-looking jeans and a bulky dark brown sweater. Now the two of them could spend the afternoon together, and he'd have a little more time to convince her how much he wanted to tag along when she told her parents about the two of them getting married.

Married, he repeated to himself for perhaps the hundredth time since making an official commitment to Lanie. He still couldn't believe he wanted to get married. Still couldn't believe how happy the thought of being married to Lanie made him feel. Obviously he'd been the marrying kind after all. He just hadn't met the right woman. But it hadn't taken any time at all for him to realize how perfect Lanie was for him.

And he couldn't wait until they started their life together for real.

They'd decided to go ahead and keep the Valentine's Day date for their real wedding, and to keep the ceremony small and have it at the governor's mansion. Well, small by Fortune standards, at any rate, Miles thought fondly. There would still probably be nearly a hundred people present. Nevertheless, he and Lanie had agreed to keep the details as close as possible to what they'd stipulated in the press conference. They'd agreed on a lot of things, he remembered fondly. Well, except for the cake. That was still up in the air.

So caught up was he with thoughts of Lanie and plans for an afternoon with her that it took him a minute to change gears when he realized it wasn't her, but her father, standing on the other side of the door. He was about to say hello to the governor, however surprised he was by the man's appearance, but his greeting was prevented by the governor himself.

"What are your intentions toward my daughter?" Tom Meyers said without preamble.

It was, to put it mildly, not the question Miles had expected to hear. He narrowed his eyes in confusion. "What?"

More slowly this time, as if he were speaking to a child, the governor asked, "What are your intentions toward my daughter?"

It was trick question, Miles thought. And not just because Lanie was supposed to have already told her father what his intentions were. Miles would have thought that by now his intentions toward Lanie would be clear to anyone who looked at them together. That he loved her and intended to marry her, so that he could spend the rest of his life with her, because life without her would be pointless.

Before he could say that, however, Tom Meyers nodded resolutely, and his shoulders slumped in defeat. "That's what I was afraid of," he said. Then he held out an envelope and added, "This is for you. Just as I promised."

His confusion multiplying, Miles took the envelope from Meyers automatically. "What is it?" he asked.

"Your payment for services rendered," the governor told him. "A hundred thousand dollars, just as I promised, for going along with this pretend engagement to Lanie."

Miles couldn't believe what he was hearing. The governor had actually thought he expected this? All this time, he'd honestly believed that the only reason Miles was spending time with Lanie was because he knew there was a bucketful of money waiting for him after it was over? He was too dumbfounded to say anything, so he only glared at the governor in response.

But Tom Meyers glared right back at him. "Oh, I know it's not what you were expecting. I know you're thinking you'll get two hundred thousand now that you've told Lanie you want to marry her for real. But I never promised that. I wasn't serious. I'd have to be an awful cad to offer a man money to marry my daughter. Now, I may be a lot of things, Fortune, and I'm not always proud of my behavior. But I'm not a panderer and I would *never* use my daughter in such a way. You can have the hundred thousand for carrying out the appearance of an engagement, but not a penny more. And now I want you to leave my daughter alone. Don't try to see Lanie again."

The governor might as well have just punched him in the nose, so shocked was Miles by what the man had said. Finally finding his voice, Miles exclaimed, "What the *hell* are you talking about?" He thrust the envelope back at Tom Meyers without even opening it. "I don't want your money. I never wanted your money. I thought you were nuts—not to mention a real son of a bitch—for ever offering it to me in the first place."

Tom's expression changed drastically at that. "You're

not expecting me to pay you for pretending to be engaged to my daughter?"

"Of course not," Miles said, nearly spitting the words. "What kind of man do you think I am?"

Meyers didn't answer at first, only studied Miles in silence, as if he were weighing some matter of grave importance. Finally, though, he said, "I thought you were just like all the other men Lanie's ever dated. Shallow. Superficial. Greedy. Stupid."

"Yeah, well, lucky for you I'm the one who fell in love with her and wants to marry her," Miles said. "Lucky for you I'm the one she fell in love with, too."

Now Tom's expression went slack. "Then it's true?" he said. "You really are in love with her? You really do want to marry her?"

Miles couldn't quite halt the anxiety that wound through him at that. Something was very, very wrong here. Lanie was supposed to have already gone over all this with her father. Just where was Lanie, anyway?

"Didn't Lanie find you this morning?" he asked.

For a minute, he didn't think Tom was going to answer. Then, very slowly, the other man nodded. "She found me."

Something cold and oily slithered through Miles's belly just then, and he wasn't quite sure what to make of it. "Then the two of you talked?" he asked Tom.

The other man nodded, but again said nothing.

"She told you we're getting married? For real?" Miles asked.

Again Tom nodded, and said nothing in response.

"And what did you tell her?" Miles asked slowly.

Tom swallowed hard. "She saw the check I made out to you," he said. "And I told her what it was for."

Miles closed his eyes at that. "You didn't. You didn't let her think I'd agreed to take money to go along with your fake engagement idea."

"I did," Tom told him.

"And then you told her about the two hundred thousand, too," Miles guessed.

"I did," the governor echoed.

The words that went through Miles's head then weren't fit to say aloud. Not until he thought about Lanie again. And then he knew exactly what to say.

"I love your daughter, Mr. Meyers. I want to be with her forever."

He shrugged a little self-consciously, some of his tension easing now that he was talking about Lanie. Whatever erroneous conclusion she'd drawn about this, Miles would make her see the truth. No matter what. But first, he had to make something clear to her father.

"Neither of us planned to fall in love," he said. "Hell, we were as surprised to have it happen as anyone. But we did fall in love. And we do want to be married. I can't imagine my life without Lanie. Hell, I should pay you for the privilege of marrying her."

Tom Meyers nodded miserably. "Well, the way I left things, son, I'm not sure anything will convince Lanie that that's what you want."

"And just where did you leave her, Mr. Meyers?"

The sound Tom expelled that time was rife with misery and fear. "When she realized what had happened…what she thought had happened," he hastily said, correcting himself, "she took off. I don't know where she went, Miles. But I know she looked pretty brokenhearted."

Brokenhearted, Miles echoed to himself. Yeah, he knew

how that felt. But he also had a feeling he might know where Lanie was. And, too, he thought he might know just how to fix this.

"On second thought, Mr. Meyers—"

"Tom," the governor corrected him.

Miles smiled, albeit a little sadly. "On second thought, Tom," he said, "let me have the check. I know exactly what to do with it."

Lanie wasn't sure how Miles knew to look for her in the park where they had shared their first kiss. But that was where he found her late in the afternoon as the sun was beginning to set. She hadn't known what to do or where to go after leaving her father's office. She hadn't wanted to go to her own room at the mansion because she'd wanted to be left alone. But she couldn't go back to the hotel to face Miles. Everywhere in Austin felt too open, made her feel exposed. Everyone in town knew who she was, and she could scarcely buy a cup of coffee without someone inquiring as to her well-being. The last question she'd wanted to answer that day was "How are you?"

So, after driving aimlessly for a while, she'd suddenly found herself turning into the entrance to the park, parking her car at the exact spot where Miles had parked his. Had it only been weeks ago? Somehow Lanie felt as if she'd known Miles forever. Now she sat alone on a picnic table scarcely a hundred yards from the copse of aspens where they had embraced that day, trying to forget everything about their time together and instead remembering every last detail. Every touch, every kiss, every caress. The way Miles looked in the morning when she woke up beside him, his sleepy smile of pleasure at realizing she was in his bed. She remembered the way his eyes crinkled at the corners when he laughed, the dimple that appeared whenever he smiled. And she realized she would never, ever be able to forget him.

And now here he was, rolling his car to a halt beside hers, unfolding his big body from inside it, standing behind the open driver's side door to look at her before approaching, as if wondering what kind of reception he could expect. As much as Lanie wished she could be angry, all she felt was sad. Sad that he wasn't the man she'd thought him to be. Sad that she would love him forever anyway.

Finally, though, he must have made a decision, because he closed the car door and began to stride slowly toward her. He picked up his pace, though, as he drew nearer, until he was jogging, then running over the last twenty or thirty feet.

When he drew to a stop before her, his dark hair was mussed by the November wind, his cheeks were ruddy from the cool autumn air. Only then did Lanie notice how cold it was today. And here she sat in her sweater and jeans. Miles had on a shearling jacket but now he took it off, covered the last few steps between him and Lanie, and dropped it over her shoulders. It was warm from his body, and it carried the familiar scent of him. It made Lanie want to cry, because she feared she would never know either of those things again.

"It's freezing out here," he said as he completed the gesture.

"I hadn't noticed," she told him honestly.

"Wow. It just got even colder," he said.

She expelled a single, humorless chuckle. "Well, how the hell am I supposed to react?" she demanded. "How am I supposed to feel when I find out the only reason you've been spending time with me is because my father was paying you? That the only reason you asked me to marry you was so that you could make even more? Well, the joke's on you, isn't it, Miles? My dad was only kidding about the two hundred thousand. Ha-ha-ha. You're stuck with a lousy hundred grand. Hope you don't feel gypped."

"I wouldn't call what I'm feeling 'gypped,'" he told her in a voice that was quiet, flat and sad.

"Yeah, well, I guess a hundred grand is a hundred grand. Better than nothing."

"It *is* nothing," he told Lanie. "Without you, a hundred grand might as well be…" He lifted one shoulder and let it drop, then reached into the pocket of his jeans to withdraw what looked like a handful of confetti. "Might as well be nothing," he said as he sifted the tiny scraps of paper to the ground. A cold gust of wind caught them and scattered them even more, carrying them across the grass to heaven knew where.

Not that Lanie cared, but she asked, "What was that?"

"That was the check your father gave to me," he told her. "He came to the hotel to deliver it after you left him this afternoon. He told me what you all talked about while you were there."

"Do you deny he offered you money to pretend to be engaged to me?" she asked.

"No," he told her, surprising her. "He did offer me money for that. And he offered me even more to marry you."

"So how much was the check he gave you today?" Lanie asked hollowly. Not that she cared about that, either.

"It could have been a billion dollars, Lanie," Miles told her, "and I still would have torn it up. I never wanted money for being with you. That wasn't why I agreed to go along with the phony engagement."

"Then why did you do it?" she asked.

He sighed heavily, then, without asking permission, climbed up onto the picnic table to sit beside her. He kept a few inches between them, though, and Lanie told herself she was glad.

Very softly, he said, "I told myself at the time that I was doing it for you."

"Oh, my, aren't you gallant," she said, striving for sarcasm, but only sounding sad.

"But eventually," he continued, ignoring the comment, "I realized I did it for me, too. Because I wanted to be with you."

She met his gaze levelly, but said nothing. He must have taken it as encouragement, because he did scoot closer to her then, until their legs were barely touching. He didn't try to touch her anywhere else, though, and Lanie told herself she was glad.

"I liked you, Lanie, from that first night we spent talking," he said quietly. "Before everything blew up in our faces, I'd planned to ask you out. Then when your father came up with this cockamamy scheme…" He sighed again. "I did it because I wanted to be with you. And then, being with you, I fell in love with you."

Tentatively, he draped an arm over her shoulders and waited to see what she would do. Lanie told herself to move away from him, but she discovered that she very much wanted to lean into him instead. So, just the littlest bit, she did.

"What I feel for you has nothing to do with money," he said softly, sounding very, very relieved. "I don't want to marry you because your father said he would pay me to. I want to marry you because I love you. More than I have ever loved anyone. I can't imagine my life without you. I don't want a life without you. No matter what you decide, whether you marry me or not, I will always love you. There will never be anyone else. Not for all the money in the world. Not for all the tea in China. Not for all the stars in the sky. Not for anything. You, Lanie. I only want you. Because I love you. It's that simple.

"I thought your father was a real jerk that day," he added. "Offering me money to spend time with his daughter. But now I'm more grateful to him than I've ever been to anyone. Because he gave me something so much more valuable than money. He gave me the chance to meet you. To get to know you. To fall in love with you. And I only hope that you will give me a second chance to prove just how much." He sighed again, with melancholy this time. "I guess if you want to go back to making our wedding bogus, I'll understand. But I will never, ever stop loving you."

Lanie turned to look at Miles fully then, noting the earnestness in his stance and the desperation in his eyes. He meant every word he'd said, she realized. He loved her. The way she loved him. Because she couldn't imagine her life without him, either, and there was nothing that could keep her away.

"Make the wedding bogus again?" she said. "Call it off? After all the planning we've done? After spending two hours getting registered at Neiman's? After the way I've fallen head over heels in love with you? I don't think so, Miles Fortune. I'm through pretending. I want the real thing now."

Throwing herself into his arms, she kissed him with all her might, with all her soul, with all her heart. With all the love she felt for him, which was almost more than her heart could hold.

Almost.

But then Miles kissed her back the same way, and she realized her heart was filling even more. As the sun dipped low over the aspens, the wind kicked up and shook free more golden leaves. Lanie watched them fall as she snuggled closer to Miles, wrapping an arm around him and pulling him close. He was hers. For real. Forever.

She couldn't believe her good fortune.

* * * * *

Everything you love about romance...
and more!

Please turn the page for Signature Select™
Bonus Features.

Bonus Features:

BONUS FEATURES

The Debutante

Author Interview:

A conversation with
ELIZABETH BEVARLY

*USA TODAY bestselling author Elizabeth Bevarly
has written more than fifty works of contemporary
romance. Recently, she chatted with us as she took a*
4 *break from writing her latest book.*

**Tell us a bit about how you began your writing
career.**

For as long as I can remember, I always wanted to
be a writer. But it was several years after earning
my B.A. in English before I finally knuckled down
and got serious about it. At that time, I was
working in retail at a Cherry Hill, New Jersey, mall
and feeling very homesick for the Caribbean,
where I lived briefly after getting married. I
started writing one cold, wet day about a
fictitious—but very warm and sunny—Caribbean
island, and gradually, it became my first book,
Destinations South, which sold to Silhouette
Special Edition. I wrote on the bus, in the food

court at the mall during lunch, in the storeroom behind the trousers on my breaks, wherever I could find time and a place to do it.

Was there a particular person, place or thing that inspired this story?
The Debutante came about when Silhouette Books invited me to take part in THE FORTUNES OF TEXAS: REUNION continuity, which means the characters and story were developed by the editors, who then presented them to me for my own personal spin. I love doing continuities because it's fun to take an "assignment" like that and make it my own. And I had a terrific time with Lanie because she gave me a chance to get in touch with my inner debutante. Growing up middle-class, I didn't have many chances to party the way she does or wear the clothes that she prefers. And she looks faboo in bright colors and sparkly jewelry, which, alas, I can't say is true for myself.

What's your writing routine?
I try to keep regular hours as much as I can. I'm usually at the computer by ten in the morning (after breakfast and light aerobics), and I write until almost three, when my son gets out of school. I usually take the weekends off, but if I'm on a deadline, I'll occasionally cram in hours on Saturday and Sunday. If I'm REALLY on deadline,

you'll see me with my laptop at my son's swim practice or karate class. Normally, though, I try to treat writing as I would any other job.

How do you research your stories?
Mostly online. I love the Internet for that. You can use Google for anything and have almost everything you need for a novel. I'm also a HUGE magazine buyer, and have stacks of them all over the house—lifestyle, decorating, travel, you name it. I love men's interest magazines most of all, because they always offer a nice insight into the male animal. And if I have a character with an unusual job, or a career I don't know much about, I'll do my best to talk to someone who does that for a living.

How you do develop your characters?
I don't really consciously develop them. They just sort of show up in my brain fully formed. When I'm writing about characters, it's really as if I'm writing about someone I met and whom I'm remembering. I think as writers, we absorb EVERYTHING we come into contact with, whether consciously or unconsciously. And then, when we sit down to write, we go to that little filing cabinet in our heads and pull what we need from several different places. I don't doubt for a moment that the woman I visualized as Lanie for *The Debutante* was probably someone I waited on

when I worked in retail, and Miles Fortune was probably some guy I served when I tended bar. I think my subconscious kept a mental picture of real people and their personalities, and then when I needed characters, there they both were.

When you're not writing, what are your favorite activities?

Well, reading, of course. I love movies, but don't get to go as often as I used to. I like to take walks. I'm a major recreational shopper—where others groan at the thought of Christmas shopping, I offer to do my mom's in addition to my own. But, honestly, more than anything else, I just love spending time with my husband and son.

If you don't mind, could you tell us a bit about your family?

I've been married for eighteen years to a guy I fell in love with in high school, and we have an almost-eleven-year-old son who is funny, smart, creative, articulate and adorable. We live a pretty quiet life, but do spend a lot of time together. I love taking walks with my son in the evenings when it's warm, and I love to cook with my husband when we can take the time to do it right. My mom is wonderful in every way, and she and I are very close. I lost my dad to Alzheimer's in 2001, something that hit my family very hard. I have two older brothers, both married, and three gorgeous, talented, funny, brilliant nieces whom I also adore.

What are your favorite kinds of vacations? Where do you like to travel?
Two words: The beach. I love, love, love going to the beach. I don't much like swimming in the ocean, but I like to wade through the water, and can walk for miles along the shore. I also like to just sit in the sand and watch the water. It is SO soothing, and so comforting and relaxing. But I enjoy visiting big cities with my husband and son, too. Chicago is a favorite place for all of us.

Do you have a favorite book or film?
My favorite film, hands down, is *Harold and Maude*. I've seen it dozens of times. I swear, that movie was the only thing that got me through my teenage years without my throwing myself off a bridge. I just love it. My favorite book—at least, the one I go back to read and reread over and over again—is *The Tao of Pooh* by Benjamin Hoff. As for novels, my favorites are *Katherine* by Anya Seton, *It Had To Be You* by Susan Elizabeth Phillips and *Lord of Scoundrels* by Loretta Chase.

Any last words to your readers?
Just a big ol' THANK YOU for reading my books! I can't tell you how grateful I am to be able to make a living doing something I love, something

that enables me to spend so much time with my family. I really, really, really appreciate all the support and enthusiasm and kind words I've received from readers and booksellers over the years. It's just incredibly nice to know that there are people out there having as much fun reading my books as I have writing them.

Don't miss Elizabeth Bevarly's novella in Write It Up!, *available from Signature Select in January 2006.*

Fortunes Trivia

How much do you know about the Fortune family? Test your knowledge by answering the following questions. Have fun and good luck!

1. Upon what occasion was Ryan Fortune's grandson Bryan kidnapped?

2. Who was behind the kidnapping of Bryan Fortune and the murder of Ryan Fortune's second wife, Sophia?

3. What evidence linked Lily Cassidy to Sophia Fortune's murder?

4. Where was King Fortune raised?

5. What are the names of King Fortune's adoptive parents?

6. Who helped Clint Lockhart after he escaped from prison?

7. To what country was Teddy Fortune, Ryan Fortune's brother, taken when he was kidnapped as a boy in 1942?

8. Who was responsible for stealing two-year-old Teddy Fortune?

9. Who gave birth to baby Taylor, the little boy rescued by the FBI and mistaken as kidnapped baby Bryan Fortune?

10. How is Matthew Fortune the father of baby Taylor?

11. What is the name of Teddy Fortune's horse ranch in New South Wales, Australia?

12. What distinctive birthmark do all the Fortunes have?

13. Why did Ryan Fortune's long-lost sister leave home at the age of seventeen?

14. What was the stipulation in Cameron Fortune's will regarding his son Holden?

15. What is the name of the boutique that wedding planner Hannah Cassidy owned?

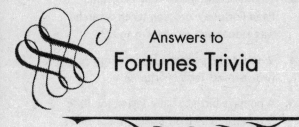

Answers to
Fortunes Trivia

1. Bryan Fortune was abducted on his christening day.

2. Clint Lockhart stole Ryan Fortune's grandchild and murdered Ryan's wife.

3. Lily's tennis bracelet, which was planted at the scene of the crime by Clint Lockhart, linked her to Sophie's murder.

4. King Fortune was raised on a pig farm in Iowa.

5. Dora and Hobart Fortune adopted King Fortune.

6. Betsy Keene helped Clint Lockhart after his prison escape.

7. Teddy Fortune was taken to Australia after his kidnapping.

8. King Fortune's father-in-law/Teddy Fortune's maternal grandfather Josiah Talbot kidnapped Teddy.

9. Maria Cassidy is baby Taylor's biological mother.

10. When Matthew Fortune was in medical school he made a donation to the sperm bank, which Maria Cassidy stole and used to secretly impregnate herself.

11. The Crown Peak is the name of Teddy Fortune's horse ranch in New South Wales, Australia.

12. King Fortune's descendants have a small crown-shaped birthmark.

13. Ryan Fortune's sister Miranda left the ranch to run off to Hollywood to become a movie star.

14. In order to receive his inheritance, Cameron Fortune's son Holden had to be married to a woman of good repute.

15. Lily Cassidy's daughter Hannah owned a boutique called The Perfect Occasion.

Here's a sneak peek...

14

Keeping Her Safe
by
Myrna Mackenzie

You won't want to miss the continuation of
THE FORTUNES OF TEXAS: REUNION, *a 12-book*
continuity series featuring the powerful Fortune family.
Enjoy this excerpt of Myrna Mackenzie's
KEEPING HER SAFE, *the seventh book in the series—*
available December 2005.

CHAPTER 1

Natalie McCabe stared up at the massive dark-haired man standing in the doorway to her apartment and wondered what she had gotten herself into. The man blocked the light from the hallway. His intense gray eyes and sharp-edged jaw were practically predatory. He looked very much like trouble, and right now she already had enough trouble in her life.

"You're not Vincent Fortune, are you?" she asked, unable to hide her concern.

"None other," he answered in a lazy voice. "Is there a problem with that?" He glanced down at her and then beyond her into her apartment.

Yes, there's a major problem, Natalie wanted to say, even as she bit her tongue. When Daniel Fortune, San Antonio's assistant district attorney, had told her he was going to assign her a bodyguard, she supposed that she had expected someone big—just not someone whose eyes took in so much. Within two seconds of opening the door, she would swear the man had registered every aspect of her house and every inch of her person. A shiver of awareness ran through her. This was a man who was used to being in control.

If there was one thing Natalie couldn't deal with, it was having someone else trying to take her control away.

"Of course there's no problem," she finally said, trying to calm herself.

The man looked down, and Natalie realized that she had clenched one fist. "I've been hired to protect you," Vincent said more gently.

"Yes, I understand that it's a necessity. I'm okay with that," she finally said.

The man looked amused, as if sensing her lie. "Mind if I come in, then?"

16 Natalie thought about that for two whole seconds. There was no way she was letting Vincent Fortune into her apartment. It wasn't just that he was big. He was also handsome with a killer smile and a low, sandy voice that promised carnal pleasure. Men like that were the kind that many women allowed favors. Women in those circumstances gave up more power than they should. Because they were lusting, not thinking.

Natalie was always thinking. Right now she was thinking that she had no business toying with the word *carnal*.

"Is it really necessary for you to come in?" she asked, desperately hoping the man couldn't read minds. "Aren't you just supposed to sit outside my house in a parked car watching for danger? Isn't that how it works?"

He raised one dark brow, not smiling. When he looked down at her, Natalie felt small and frail, even though she wasn't either of those things. At five-six she wasn't short, and she visited a club regularly and had taken self-defense courses.

"You and I need to establish a working relationship and some basic ground rules before I can decide what the best course of action is, Ms. McCabe," the man said. "To do that we need to sit down and talk, and you probably don't want to talk in a place where anyone can overhear us."

Okay, he had a point. Natalie took a deep breath, her options fading. Not for the first time she wished her situation were different. When she had been assigned to cover the party the governor had thrown to honor noted philanthropist and head of the Fortune family Ryan Fortune for his contributions to charity, it had been an ordinary day. Just as usual, her boss at the *San Antonio Express-News* had stuck her with the social circuit when she wanted the chance to cover hard news stories.

Then she had witnessed Jason Jamison murdering his wife, and everything had changed. She was no longer just a reporter but also a witness to a crime.

Not long ago her tires had been slashed, and recently she had begun receiving threatening notes. She needed protection, and Daniel Fortune was convinced that his brother Vincent ran the best security firm available. Damn!

"I don't mean to be a pain, Mr. Fortune," Natalie said, still not inviting him in, "but exactly how do I know that you're who you say you are? Especially given my situation, I can't just invite a stranger into my house."

Vincent nodded slightly. His eyes crinkled at the corners in a way that made Natalie's stomach flutter. *Don't be stupid,* she told herself.

"You've just become my favorite client, Ms. Mc-Cabe," Vincent Fortune was saying. "Most people let me in without asking any tough questions. I'll show you my credentials, but I'd also advise that you call my brother just to make sure that I am who I am. That way you'll have some peace of mind."

Which was such a joke. She hadn't had peace of mind since this whole Jason Jamison business had started. Moreover, she was currently involved in some sensitive sleuthing for an article she wanted—no, needed—to write, and having someone trailing her would be a decided disadvantage. Besides, this man, with his short dark hair, gray eyes and hard-muscled body, was not the kind to make any woman feel peaceful. Unless one counted the afterglow of a sexual encounter as peaceful...

"I'll call Daniel," she said, chasing her thoughts away as she pulled out her cell phone and dialed Daniel's number.

18

"Hi, Natalie," Daniel said when she had told him what she wanted. "Yes, that's definitely my big brother. He's a bit imposing, but I can assure you that he's highly effective."

Natalie looked up, and her eyes met Vincent's. For a minute she couldn't look away, couldn't swallow. *Imposing* was a good word for the man. It was a word she didn't much care for.

"Are you okay with this, Natalie?" Daniel asked. "I don't mean to scare you, but until Jamison's case is complete, and with these notes circulating, you need to be protected. Vincent will do that. He's more dependable than anyone I know, and he's capable, as well. He'll get the job done. All right?"

No, she was not all right. For years she had been treated as a cute but inept little doll by her family. Moreover, Joe Franklin, her good-old-boy boss, felt that women should be happy just to write fluff pieces. Now Vincent Fortune would join the ranks of those who wanted to protect little Natalie McCabe from the world. He would smother her with his undeniable presence. But she had no choice. To change things she had to remain healthy and alive.

"I'm fine with that, Daniel. Thank you." She hung up.

"All right, come in and let's get started, Mr. Fortune," she said, stepping back and letting the man in her doorway inside. "But I'm going to be honest.

I'm really uncomfortable having a man following me around."

"Excuse me," he said, "but I have to ask. Is it just the prospect of having a bodyguard that bothers you or the fact that I'm a man?" His eyes turned dark and he didn't surge forward into her house as she would have expected. "Because," he continued, "you should understand that most people are uncomfortable having a shadow at first. They get used to it. If the discomfort goes deeper, though, I need to know."

She felt herself growing warm. "I just don't like feeling helpless. Having someone paid to keep me safe makes me feel hemmed in, frustrated. I have work to do, Mr. Fortune." It was important work, too. The story she was trying to uncover would not only help establish her as a respected reporter, but it would bring justice to many elderly people who had been wronged. She couldn't give that up.

Vincent gave her a curt nod. "I respect your work, Ms. McCabe. I hope *you* understand that while VF Securities is my business, and I take pride in my work, this situation goes beyond that. I take the intimidation of innocent individuals very seriously. That's what I'm seeing here. You've been threatened. I've seen the notes that have been sent to you. Someone wants to frighten you. He or she wants you out of the picture. I don't intend to let that happen."

Suddenly the thing she had been avoiding thinking about came rushing back at her. *I'm watching you, Natalie. You're never alone, Natalie. Don't let down your guard, Natalie.* The notes had frightened her a great deal, it was true. Her hands had trembled just holding the bits of paper those notes had been written on, and she felt sick even remembering those moments. But giving in to that fear, letting someone else take away her choice to be strong and to be the one in charge… It just made the fear worse in a way. She had struggled all her life for the chance to follow her own path. This was too much like admitting that her family had been right all along, like conceding that she really was weak, parasitically helpless.

The thought threatened to overwhelm her, suffocate her. She gave herself a mental shake and tried to stand taller. "Mr. Fortune, I grew up with parents and three older brothers who felt I was incapable of even walking across the street without assistance. I *do* understand the need for your expertise and your protection, and I *am* grateful for all you and Daniel are trying to do for me. But I have to be able to live my life and do my job without interference. I have to be able to have some semblance of normalcy."

"All right," he said in his dark, sexy voice as he entered her home and shut the door behind him. "I'll do all I can to make that possible. I'm here to watch your back, and I'll do my best to make it easy for you."

But as he brushed past her, and she caught a whiff of his aftershave, a fragrance that only emphasized

SNEAK PEEK BONUS FEATURE

his masculinity, she couldn't imagine it ever being easy to have this man watching her every move. Already she felt as if she was walking around in her underwear. His eyes were everywhere. She could see him assessing every nook and cranny of her living room, noting the locks on the windows, the open curtains that let in the sunshine.

She could almost hear her parents clucking every time she took a risk. She could remember her three brothers' frowns if a boy so much as glanced below her neck. This kind of scrutiny was not new to her. The old, familiar sense of beating her head against the wall crept right back in, only this time she couldn't pretend the scrutiny was unjustified, that she could handle everything on her own. Like it or not, someone really was threatening her.

22

"I appreciate your candor and your promises, but my life *is* going to change, isn't it?" she asked softly.

"Yes," he said, turning to face her with a sad nod. "It already has. You were in the wrong place at the wrong time, and because of that everything will be different from here on out."

"Some people would say I was in the right place at the right time. Jason Jamison is behind bars."

He gave a slight nod. "Yes."

But Natalie had to admit that his first comment had been right in a way. Because she was a valued witness whose safety was in question, she was going to be spending a lot of time with a man she wouldn't ordinarily have ever met, one she would never have chosen to meet.

Natalie sighed and nodded. "All right, keep me safe, Mr. Fortune."

"It will be my primary goal."

And hers would be to keep her life as normal as possible, to make sure that Vincent Fortune remained a shadow, one she could shed once this mess with Jason Jamison was over.

...NOT THE END...

Look for Keeping Her Safe *by Myrna Mackenzie in stores December 2005.*

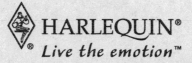

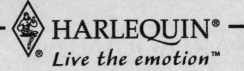

HARLEQUIN®
Live the emotion™

eHARLEQUIN.com

The Ultimate Destination for Women's Fiction

Your favorite authors are just a click away
at www.eHarlequin.com!

- Take a sneak peek at the covers and
  read summaries of **Upcoming Books**

- Choose from over 600
  author **profiles!**

- Chat with your favorite authors
  on our **message boards.**

- Are you an author in the making?
  Get advice from published authors
  in **The Inside Scoop!**

**Learn about your favorite authors
in a fun, interactive setting—
visit www.eHarlequin.com today!**

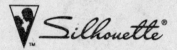